A Royal

Eileen Dunlop

A Royal Ring of Gold

Stories from the Life of Mungo

Floris Books

Illustrations by Georgina McBain

First published in 1999 by Floris Books

The publisher gratefully acknowledges
subsidy from the Scottish Arts Council
towards the publication of this book.

British Library CIP Data available

ISBN 0-86315-292-9

Printed in Great Britain
by Cromwell Press, Trowbridge, Wilts.

For Connie,
and in memory of
Dr Peter Brodie,
my minister at St Mungo's, Alloa
1947–86

Contents

Author's note

Although St Kentigern, or Mungo, is the patron saint of Glasgow and has churches named after him in Scotland, Cumbria and Wales, nothing much is really known about him. He was probably a Briton who worked as a Christian missionary in Strathclyde and Cumbria, and there is a strong tradition that he was a bishop and founder of the church at Glasgow. He is said to have died on 13 January, probably in AD 614. His tomb is a feature of Glasgow Cathedral. All the best known stories about him are clearly legends, and there is a good reason why.

For almost six hundred years after Mungo's death, stories about him were spread only by word of mouth. Some true things were forgotten and, in attempts to make good stories even better, incidents that never actually happened were added on. By 1184, when Joscelin, a monk from Furness in Lancashire, began to write Mungo's life story, it had become impossible to separate truth from legend.

No one nowadays regards Joscelin's Life of St Kentigern, on which *A Royal Ring of Gold* is based, as historical. It is a collection of wonderful stories, some echoing Irish legends, others interweaving with the legends of King Arthur. They are a tribute to a much loved saint and part of Scotland's rich storytelling tradition.

1. Theneu's Story

Theneu crouched in the bottom of the coracle, stiff with cold in her sleeveless woollen dress. Too tired even to cry, she listened to the waves pawing the fragile, hide-covered shell. If only, she thought, she had no one but herself to consider, how little she would mind being washed over the side into the black water. To be numbed and sink down into forgetfulness — after so much suffering, what a blessed release that would be. But Theneu was not alone. Inside her there was a baby. For his — or her — sake, Theneu knew that she must try to stay alive, although she refused to pray to a God whom she believed had deserted her.

Darkness and danger made every moment seem like an hour. Theneu felt as if she had been afloat for many days. Yet she knew that since she'd left the shore at Aberlessic, the sun had gone down only once. She had watched it teetering like a bright hoop on the western hills before toppling down suddenly against a blood-stained sky. As night revealed the stars, Theneu had feared that the tide might drag the oarless boat out of the great river mouth into the open sea. It was a relief, as the moon rose, still to make out on her left the outline of the shore from which she'd come. An even greater relief was to see another shore to her right. Theneu and her baby were floating up river. The tide was taking her inland.

A full moon scattered mercury on the water. Exhausted and thankful that she wasn't after all drifting towards the rim of a flat world, Theneu longed to sleep. Yet every time her heavy eyes closed, she started awake again. Fear of dreaming kept her wakeful, although she knew that nightmares weren't confined to sleep. However much she wanted to, Theneu couldn't prevent the poisonous snake of memory from loosening its coils in her mind.

Until a year ago, Theneu remembered, she had been happy. The only daughter of a powerful king called Loth, she had lived all her short life in a great wooden-walled fortress on a high hill called Dun Paladyr. Theneu loved the view from the battlements, the windy sky and the wet plain tumbling in green waves towards the distant sea. On the landward side there was forest. Thickly leaved in summer, like grey smoke in winter, it leant towards hills softened by fine rain. Dun Paladyr was a wonderful place for seeing rainbows.

Life was hard in many ways, even for a princess. Motherless since early childhood, Theneu slept in a draughty thatched hut with all the other unmarried women of the king's household. She spent tedious hours spinning and weaving in a stuffy, ill-lit room. In winter, when icicles hung like long teeth from the thatch and the wind roared from the sea, Theneu suffered as many colds and chilblains as the kitchen maid or the kennel boy.

Of course, there were compensations. Because she was the king's daughter, Theneu had fine dresses to wear, dyed yellow as saffron, purple as blaeberry juice. She had silver bracelets, necklaces and combs, and a gold brooch to fasten her fur-lined cloak. In summer she had a pony to ride and enjoyed wild gallops towards the shining sea.

Theneu had never thought much about religion, except at the four great festivals of the year, when she joined her father in feasting and worshipping the ancient gods of her people. Theneu loved King Loth's great hall, with its embroidered hangings and weapons gleaming in the firelight. She loved listening to the bards striking their harps and chanting tales of heroes long ago. And although she hated the fierce bonfires lit to honour the baleful gods, and was afraid of their priests, the scowling, spell-muttering druids, she felt safe because her father was nearby.

More than anyone in the world Theneu loved King Loth, with his golden beard and ringing laugh, and his casual fondness for dogs and children. Of course, now and then, she saw him in a temper, raging and stamping through the house while his servants cowered and trembled like flames in the wind. But she never thought he could be angry with her. That was until she was sixteen and Sister Brignat came into her life. As the coracle rocked like a cradle on the waves, Theneu's heart ached at the memory of Brignat, whose happiness she had destroyed as surely as Brignat had destroyed hers.

Theneu never understood why her father had allowed six nuns, holy women dedicated to prayer and worship of the new God of the Christians, to settle at Dun Paladyr. Loth was not a Christian, and only half believed in any gods at all. But he was generous in an offhand way, and no doubt Moninne, the nuns' first leader, was persuasive. Loth gave permission for a tiny settlement called a convent, consisting of six thatched huts like beehives and a small wooden church, to be built on a rocky spur some distance from the fortress. Moninne, always restless, departed to found convents elsewhere, leaving Brignat in charge. The nuns lived discreetly behind their wattle fence and Loth forgot about them.

Theneu, although she liked to hear the convent bell throwing its frail chimes against the wind, took no interest in the nuns. If she ever thought about them, it was to shudder at the notion of wearing a hairy brown shift and a scratchy headcloth, and staying up all night to pray. As for the nuns' vow never to marry, because husband and children would interfere with their duty to God, Theneu found it incomprehensible. Her ambition was to marry a handsome young chieftain and be the mother of happy children. If only she had been true to it, she wouldn't be lost, abandoned and in peril now.

It was a sultry summer afternoon. Crickets chirped in the grass and pears were ripening along the convent fence. Theneu had ridden out alone, as she often did, to exercise her pony. On the way home, startled by a rabbit darting across the path, the pony reared and threw Theneu into the ditch outside the convent gate. Two nuns, round-faced and clucking like motherly hens, ran from their tiny garden to help her.

"Take my hand, my dear. Up you come! What a naughty pony!"

"Come to Sister Brignat, child. She'll take care of you."

Winded and limping slightly, Theneu allowed herself to be led inside the woven fence. Sister Brignat, alerted by the commotion, came out quietly from her beehive cell. Theneu saw a thin brown face and dark eyes made more intense by the whiteness of a woollen headcloth. Brignat's manner was cool, but her long fingers were gentle as they put ointment on Theneu's skinned knees and examined her head, arms and legs.

"No bones broken, Princess," she said eventually, adding, "I'm afraid your pony has run home without you. Shall I walk with you to your father's gate?"

Theneu wasn't surprised to be recognized. She was dressed like a princess, after all. What surprised her was her own reply.

"No, thank you. But before I go home, may I see inside your church?"

Had it been curiosity that made her ask, she wondered, as she shivered in the wet bottom of the coracle. Or had she even then been in the power of some evil god who wanted to harm her? Certainly she had no real interest in the rough hut towards which Sister Brignat politely ushered her. And yet — Theneu would never forget the mysterious sense of homecoming she experienced as she stepped over the threshold. There was a summery scent of freshly strewn rushes and, through the windowless gloom, she could make out a tiny altar. On it stood a wooden cross and two flickering lamps.

"There isn't much to see, but God sees us," said Sister Brignat.

On the eastern horizon, the sun ran a silver finger along the sea. The stars drew back, but Theneu, with her face buried in her hands, didn't see the promise of a new day. With bitter love she was remembering Brignat, who had told her about the Christian God — had told her, she now believed, nothing but lies.

At the time, it had all seemed wonderful. Drawn by the peace of the little church and Brignat's glorious stories, Theneu slipped away as often as she could from the stir and clamour of King Loth's stronghold. She knelt on the hard floor of the church, listening to the nuns' joyful Psalms:

> *Praise him, hills and mountains,*
> *Fruit trees and forests,*
> *all animals tame and wild,*
> *reptiles and birds.*
> *Praise him, kings and all peoples...*

She accompanied Brignat into the forest to visit the poor, malnourished people who huddled in shelters under the trees. She watched as Brignat tended their sores and gave them food which the nuns could ill afford. Theneu was afraid at first, but Brignat was afraid of nothing.

> *The Lord is faithful to his promises,*
> *and everything he does is good.*
> *He helps those who are in trouble,*
> *He lifts those who have fallen.*

Theneu fell in love with this God who had made the world beautiful and cared for all its creatures — unlike the old gods who were worshipped only for fear of the darkness they represented. But she never even thought of being a nun herself until Prince Owain arrived at Dun Paladyr to claim her as his wife.

It was very sad, really. A year earlier, Prince Owain would have seemed the fulfilment of all Theneu's dreams. He was handsome in a rough, hairy way, and no vainer than King Loth, who swaggered a lot in his plaid tunic and admired his own whiskers in a polished bronze mirror. Prince Owain was less smelly than most men and his manners were reasonable. He went behind the fence to urinate and, if he had drunk too much, he left the great hall before he was sick. He smiled boyishly at Theneu, although he was at least fifteen years older than she was. He seemed genuinely anxious that she would like the gifts he had brought.

"The brooch was my mother's, so I hope you'll enjoy wearing it. My sister made the cloak. Do you like the colour? The blue matches your eyes and goes so well with your lovely golden hair."

Theneu couldn't have asked for more. So why was it

that she shrank from Owain's touch and turned her face away when he tried, quite gently, to kiss her?

"I can't bear him," she said bluntly to Sister Brignat one autumn morning, as they walked together under the trees. "I don't want to marry him, and the law of our people says I can't be forced. I want to be a nun and serve God, like you."

Theneu expected Brignat to be pleased. She was disappointed to see a troubled expression on her friend's sallow face. But Brignat's answer was resolute enough.

"If that's your true desire, Theneu, you must tell your father that you can't marry Prince Owain. Only ..."

"Only what, Sister?"

"Only be sure you know what you're doing. Our life is very hard, and your choosing it will cause great suffering, not only to yourself."

Even with this warning, Theneu couldn't have begun to imagine the horror of the storm which engulfed her. Now it was she who cowered as King Loth rampaged through the hall and the courtyard, throwing plates and wine cups, swearing and kicking every living thing unfortunate enough to come within range of his large foot.

"You ungrateful little pig!" he bawled, his face purple with rage. "How dare you go against my wishes and ruin my alliance with Prince Owain? Get out of my house!"

He tore off Theneu's jewellery with brutal hands. As for Prince Owain, his pouting, crestfallen expression would have been almost funny had it not been succeeded by a wolfish, vengeful look which terrified Theneu.

"I've nothing against you," she tried to tell him, but he turned away with an angry snarl.

The days that followed were terrible. As the wind turned into the east and frost-nipped leaves blew over the hill, Theneu was turned out-of-doors in her shift. She didn't go to the convent, for fear of getting the nuns into trouble, but sought shelter instead with the poor wretches who lived in the forest. From them she learned something terrible. The nuns were gone, expelled at sword-point by Loth's soldiers, their convent smashed and hurled down the hillside. As she wept, Theneu seemed to hear their sweet voices singing:

> *Lord, let me live in your sanctuary all my life;*
> *Let me find safety under your wings.*
> *You have heard my promises, o God,*
> *and you have given me what belongs*
> *to those who honour you.*

Lies, all lies, thought Theneu bitterly, as she huddled under a tattered deerskin in a hovel among the trees. There was even worse to come.

The man who had given Theneu shelter was called Henn. Compared with his neighbours he was rich, because he owned two pigs. When, one frosty morning, one of the pigs ran away, Henn called everyone to help look for it. Theneu, of course, joined the hunt. Quite soon, however, the voices of her companions faded and she found herself in an unfamiliar part of the forest. Theneu was beyond fear. Indeed, she rather liked the bare branches lacing the pale sky and the silence broken only by the conversation of birds.

The attack came suddenly — a twig snapping underfoot, a harsh parting of the undergrowth, a hand over Theneu's mouth while another clawed eagerly at her body. Theneu tried to struggle, but in vain. She was thrown down violently on the cold ground, her mouth stopped by wet, bearded lips. Bony fingers tore frantically at her clothing, scratching her arms and breasts.

Mercifully Theneu lost consciousness then, but when she came round, bruised and bleeding, she knew exactly what had happened to her. She also knew her attacker. It was Prince Owain.

The forest folk went on sheltering her for nine long months, while a baby grew inside her. But they didn't talk to her and even the kindest looked askance, as if what had happened was her own fault. She never knew which of them informed King Loth that she was pregnant, though she suspected Henn, who had lost a pig and might hope for a reward. It didn't really matter.

At dawn — could it only have been yesterday? — soldiers had come through the wood and arrested her. Trussed up in a cart, she was dragged past her childhood home at Dun Paladyr and bumped over long, stony tracks to the sea. Rough hands untied her and forced her into a coracle; although she was obviously ready to give birth, she was given neither food, fresh water nor an oar.

"Orders of King Loth," were the last words Theneu heard, as men with poles thrust the flimsy boat out into the deep water.

As daylight crept from the east, Theneu felt a jolt and realized that the coracle had run aground. Raising her head, she saw a grey, muddy shore creeping towards a scarf of scrubby woodland. Somehow, she dragged herself out of the coracle and began to stumble up the beach.

2. Bullies

"Mungo! Mungo!"

"Little doggie!"

"Teacher's pet!"

The mocking voices were pitched low for fear of being overheard, but they were as insistent as the wind above the mud-flats. Curled up on the straw mattress in his little thatched cell, Mungo wondered how much more of this treatment he could stand. He wasn't physically afraid of his fellow pupils. They wouldn't dare to attack him and, even if they did, he was big and brave enough now to defend himself. It was their hatred and jealousy that made him feel sick, especially since it was jealousy of things he couldn't control.

"Little doggie!"

"Woof! Woof!"

"Teacher's pet!"

"Go away!" protested Mungo, but instead of the growl he'd intended the words came out high and squeaky. Mungo pushed his fingers into his ears to shut out his tormentors' delighted sniggers.

Most nights the taunting went on for a long time, until the bullies got bored and drifted off to their own cells. But not tonight. Half irritated and half relieved, Mungo heard the low but authoritative voice of Serf, the abbot and headmaster of the monastery school.

"What are you boys doing here? Get off to bed at once. Your play time was over long ago."

Mungo heard the scamper of sandalled feet, then the sackcloth curtain which hung over the entrance to his little hut was drawn aside. Ducking his grey, balding head, Serf entered, letting in a thin shaft of late summer light. There was scarcely enough room for one person, let alone two, but Serf folded his thin body neatly onto Mungo's stool. He looked thoughtfully at his pupil's pale, tense face.

"Do you want to tell me about it?" he asked.

There was a lot Mungo wanted to tell Serf. Like that it was all his fault. Mungo had lost count of the times he'd stood cringing in front of the whole school, while Serf praised his intelligence and thanked God for the favour he had shown him. Worse still, Serf couldn't resist holding Mungo up as an example to the other boys. This was very embarrassing, because their fathers paid for them to learn reading and writing, and enough Latin to become monks themselves when they grew up. Whereas Mungo didn't pay and didn't even know who his father was. He wanted to tell the old man to shut up and stop ruining his chances of ever making friends.

But as he looked up at the kind, concerned old face, Mungo knew that he could never say such harsh things to Serf. He owed him too much. From his mother Mungo had heard, over and over again, how she had come to the shore at Cuilen Ros, "the point where holly grows," one cold dawn in an open boat. On the shore she had given birth, frightened and terribly alone. Some shepherds, alerted by the sound of a baby crying, had gone to fetch Serf, whose monastery was close at hand.

Although, as he laughingly admitted, he knew next to nothing about women and nothing at all about babies, Serf had promptly taken responsibility for both mother and child. Shelter, food and clothing were found, and it was Serf who had gradually brought Mungo's mother,

Theneu, back from the brink of madness to faith in the God who said, "I shall not leave you comfortless."

Serf had baptized the baby, giving him the name Kentigern, meaning "the high lord," which Mungo thought was funny in the circumstances. As a tiny child he had trotted everywhere after Serf and so acquired his nickname, Mungo, which had the double meaning of "dear friend" and "little dog."

Mungo had loved Serf then and he loved him now. So when the old man repeated, "Is there anything you want to tell me, Mungo?" Mungo didn't tell the whole truth.

"I don't think the other boys like the things I can do, Father," he said tightly.

Serf looked sympathetically at Mungo in the fading light.

"Life is often hard for people whom God has chosen," he said. "Think of the Bible — how jealous Esau was of his brother Jacob, and how angry Joseph's brothers were when they saw the coloured coat his father had given him. Your fellow pupils are envious in the same way. They covet the gift which God has given you."

"But I just want friends," gulped Mungo, who was only thirteen. "I want to be ordinary and have friends."

He heard Serf sigh in the gloom.

"You will have friends," he said comfortingly. "But perhaps not here. Not now."

Mungo bit his lip as Serf tucked his blanket round him and made the sign of the Cross over his head. But when the abbot was gone and he was alone in the dark, he pulled the blanket over his head and cried bitterly.

3. A Strange Power

Mungo could remember exactly when he had first realized that he had power which others didn't have. It was the Christmas after he left his mother's hut to become a pupil at the monastery school. According to the stick on which Theneu proudly notched his birthdays, he was seven years old.

Until that time, Mungo had lived with Theneu in a ramshackle village which clung to the flat, wind-raked shore of a great river. Serf called the river *Sinus Orientalis,* which was Latin for "the gulf of the east," but everyone else called it the Gwerid. Mungo didn't mind the cold, or the rain that dripped through the thatch in winter, hissing on the hearthstone and damping the thin bedding; it was all he'd ever known. He ran around happily with the neighbours' children, learning how to fish from the rocks and dig for bait in the rich, silky brown mud.

Mungo was different from his companions only in what he wanted to do when he grew up. While they looked forward to being herds and fishermen like their fathers, Mungo wanted to be a monk like his friend Serf. As a small child, he could scarcely wait to go to school. The nearby monastery, which stood behind an earthen rampart topped by a wooden fence, seemed to him like a Promised Land. Every time Abbot Serf came to visit Theneu, Mungo would tug at his robe and look up imploringly into his weatherbeaten face.

"When may I come to school, Father?" he would ask.

"When you're seven, my son," Serf would reply. Then, one wonderful spring day, the abbot at last spoke the words Mungo wanted to hear. "This year, when the leaves turn red, I shall come to fetch you."

For the first months at school, everything went well. Mungo was proud of his new brown tunic and woollen cloak, and delighted with his little cell. He liked having his own space where he could sit up late, practising writing and reading the Gospels for as long as there was oil left in his little lamp. When the wind whistled eerily around the thatch and wolves howled in the high wood Mungo missed his mother, but the words she had taught him calmed his fear.

> *The Lord will guard you;*
> *He is by your side to protect you.*
> *The sun will not hurt you during the day,*
> *Or the moon during the night.*

Although all his fellow pupils were older than he was, they were affable enough. Bewic, the head boy, even took Mungo under his wing for a while.

"He's only a little kid," Bewic pointed out when the other boys groused occasionally about Serf's favouritism. "Remember, none of us came here until we were nine."

So the boys shrugged and allowed Mungo to tag along after them. Bewic taught him to play knucklebones and he joined in games of hide-and-seek. As Christmas approached, however, this pleasant state of affairs changed.

It seemed at first that the weather was to blame. After a mild, weepy November, when the eaves dripped and fawnish fog slipped silently up and down the river, winter had come bitterly. Each morning hoar frost stiffened the grass and drew mysterious runes on gateposts and walls. Each afternoon the sun set sullen, cold and far away. Serf and his monks took the cold in their stride, but the schoolboys found it hard to bear. When Serf gave Mungo not one but two extra blankets, their goodwill towards the new boy evaporated.

"Who's a little doggie, then?"

"Teacher's pet!"

"Angel-face!"

For the first time Mungo heard the names that would haunt him through all his schooldays. The most offensive was the reference to his blue eyes and curly, golden hair. Bewic, who had a streaming cold, didn't try to defend him.

"Time you learned to watch out for yourself," he growled.

Then nasty things began to happen. An inkpot was upset on a text which Abbot Serf had given Mungo to copy. A page of his psalm-book was torn and food stolen from his wooden plate. The cloak which Theneu had woven for him as a parting gift went missing. Two days later it was thrown into his cell, ripped and smeared with mud. Mungo knew that the bigger boys wanted to get him into trouble, and were disappointed when Serf didn't punish him. He didn't cry openly, but as Christmas approached, promising little except a day's holiday from lessons and a honeycomb to sweeten the breakfast loaves, he was very unhappy.

If only, Mungo thought desperately, the weather would improve, then perhaps the mood of his companions would improve too. Instead, the weather got worse. Stinging winds blew from the east. The sky above the river was bruised and heavy with sleet. It was Christmas Eve when something really dreadful happened.

There was a tradition in the monastery that the monks were excused work on Christmas Eve, so that they could prepare to celebrate Christ's birth by fasting and praying in their cells. The schoolboys took over their duties, milking the cows, feeding the hens and cooking their own dinner on the kitchen fire. This was the only fire in the monastery, used for cooking, providing light for lamps and, once a day, unfreezing numb fingers and toes. The boys' last task on Christmas Eve was to carry burning twigs from the kitchen to the church and light the lamps which at midnight would welcome the Christ Child.

Bewic was supposed to be in charge but it was another boy, Gweir, who had smart ideas. Because Gweir was handsome and jaunty, and his father was a prince, Bewic most often did as he said.

It was late afternoon and getting dark by the time the boys had finished their dinner of fish and eggs cooked on the hot firestone. Mungo, whose share had mostly been eaten by Bewic and Gweir, had been ordered to clean the greasy wooden plates with a brush made of hazel twigs. While he was busy Gweir beckoned his companions to the other end of the kitchen. Mungo heard them whispering, but was determined not to show that he minded being left out.

There was some giggling, then Gweir said, "Listen, doggie. We're going out for a while. Can't take you, of course — dogs aren't allowed. While we're away, it'll be your job to keep the fire burning. When you hear the first strokes of the monastery bell, light a twig and carry it over to the church. Light the lamps on the altar, then scuttle away to your cell. All right?"

Of course, it wasn't all right. Mungo had never tended a fire in his life, and he quailed at the prospect of blundering through the dark, draughty church carrying such a frail yet vital light. But he knew it would be fruitless to argue, so he nodded dumbly. The boys picked up their cloaks and vanished, laughing, into the dusk.

When he had finished cleaning the plates, Mungo fetched some fuel and rather tentatively stoked the fire. He had no idea how much wood to put on. Suppose, he thought nervously, that he overdid it and set fire to the kitchen? Better to put on a little at a time, watching to make sure that the flames didn't die. With a pile of sticks beside him, he sat down on the earth floor. It was going to be a long evening.

For a while Mungo watched the fire carefully, feeding it whenever the flames died down. He tried to strengthen himself by praying, but he was hungry and terribly tired. The kitchen, with its blackened walls and smoke hanging under the sooty thatch, was stupefyingly stuffy. Try as he might, Mungo couldn't keep his eyes open. Curling up like a hedgehog, he fell fast asleep.

The first strokes of the monastery bell, rung to warn the monks that midnight was near, were heard by Mungo as though in a dream. Only at the second, more insistent ringing did he start up in the dark, gasping with horror. The hour of Christ's coming on earth had arrived. The fire was out and the church was in darkness. Mungo could have wept with shame.

Stumbling to the door, Mungo peered out into the night. The moon was peeking through a rent in the clouds. By its light he could see the monks emerging from their cells, their shadows tiny on the frosty ground. Suddenly he heard voices.

"This is your fault, Gweir."

That was Bewic, angrily accusing.

"My fault?" Gweir was furious. "How was I to know the stupid little fool would fall asleep?"

"I just hope you all enjoyed the fun and games at Godeu's place," said someone else gloomily. "We're in big trouble now."

Mungo didn't care that they were in trouble, nor that he was in trouble himself. The tears rising in his eyes were for Serf and the other monks, whose Christmas was spoiled, and for the Christ Child who would find no welcome in their church that night. Hardly knowing what he was doing, Mungo picked up a cold branch that the cook had left propped up beside the kitchen door.

In tears, he groped his way back to the hearthstone and poked forlornly at the dead embers. There wasn't even a flicker of light.

"Forgive me, God," whispered Mungo.

Then it happened. As he stood shivering, Mungo felt a surge of warmth through his thin body. The branch, for an instant, became almost too hot to hold. Its tip glowed rosily, then burst suddenly into a flower of flame. Unwavering in the draught from the open door, it shone as clear and bright as the Christmas star. Full of wonder and happiness, Mungo walked steadily across the yard to the church. The altar lamps shone out like little suns at the touch of the blessed fire.

4. The Robin

"I felt the day you were born that God had chosen you," said Serf, as he and Mungo walked back from Theneu's house on Christmas Day. "Last night's miracle proves I was right."

It was a mild, serene day, contrasting pleasantly with the recent turmoil of wind and cruel sleet. Now the sky was the colour of a duck's egg and the tide ran silver under the sun. Normally Mungo would have been darting about, picking up treasures to show to Serf, shells, feathers, softly coloured stones. But today he walked quietly with his hand in his friend's.

"Was it a miracle, Father?" he asked. "I mean — suppose the fire hadn't really gone out?"

"Do you think that's the truth?" asked Serf.

"No," admitted Mungo. "But why me?"

Serf squeezed Mungo's hand.

"I suppose everyone whom God has ever chosen has asked that question," he replied. "I know I did, when I realized God was calling me to leave my comfortable home in an eastern land. The last thing I wanted was to travel for years over mountains and across wild seas, only to end up in a bleak, cold place like this. But I found peace here, and now God has sent me a sign and a promise. I chose to be known as Serf, which means "servant," but you will be a greater servant of God than I have ever been."

Such expectation alarmed Mungo.

"But what does God want me to do, Father?" he asked anxiously.

Serf shook his head.

"I don't know, Mungo," he said. "God never shows you the whole of your life like a scroll unrolled on a table. What he wants now is for you to work hard, learn all you can and be happy. When you're older, he'll tell you what he wants you to do next."

This made sense to Mungo. He walked in silence for a while, enjoying the shore smells and the gulls' cries. But as they neared the monastery gate, he felt suddenly anxious.

"Father," he said, "you won't punish the other boys for what happened yesterday, will you?"

Serf frowned and tutted impatiently.

"They certainly deserve punishment," he said sternly. "They disobeyed me and broke my rule by visiting the house of that drunken rascal Godeu. But no, I shan't beat them this time. Without their disobedience, there would have been no miracle."

During the years that followed, Mungo did work hard and learned a great deal, but he was not happy. Although time after time his pleading with Serf saved his fellow pupils from punishment, they were never grateful. Even when Bewic and Gweir had left school, there were other boys eager to poison the minds of new pupils.

"That's Mungo. You have to watch him. He's Serf's pet and he sneaks to the monks about everyone," they lied.

Mungo bore his misery as best he could, although sometimes he cried in bed and often begged Serf to treat him like everyone else. Eventually, however, he stopped trying to make friends. He studied night and day, and waited patiently for God to unroll the next section of the scroll of his life.

Meanwhile, the power which had first surged through Mungo on Christmas Eve came and went. When he was ten, he cured the cook, Brother Caef, of a terrible fever, simply by putting his hands on the monk's head. When he was twelve, on a journey with Serf through the hills called Ochel to the north of the river, he healed a leper who was weeping by the road side. But when Mungo tried to summon the power to relight his lamp when it blew out in a draught, or to increase the size of his dinner, nothing happened. That was how he learned that the power wasn't a kind of magic; it could only be used for the good of others. Which, Mungo thought wryly, was just as well. There were times when he might have been tempted to use it to teach his nasty schoolfellows a lesson.

At last, when he was sixteen, Mungo was ready to change his schoolboy tunic for the long brown habit of a monk. It was what he had always wanted, and he had no regrets about the things he would miss — a wife and children, wealth and a home of his own. He had always assumed that he would stay on at Cuilen Ros, helping Serf and eventually taking over as abbot. He knew that was what Serf wanted too. In his last week as a pupil, however, something happened which led Mungo to revise his plans.

Just as the monks were forbidden to have families or even special friends, they were not allowed to keep pets. This was particularly hard on Serf, who loved animals and was loved by them. Whenever he visited the village, dogs ran to greet him. Theneu's cat curled up, purring ecstatically, on his knee. At the monastery, he couldn't stop birds adopting him. Sparrows, thrushes and blackbirds thronged to his cell, hopping on the roof and hoping to be fed. Most of all Serf loved a robin, who was so tame that he would perch on the old monk's finger and peck crumbs out of his beard.

To be fair, the schoolboys hadn't set out to kill the robin. But the one who had enticed it onto his hand passed it to another, then it was snatched by a third. By the time Mungo appeared round the corner of the church, the tiny creature was being tossed around like a ball. Its wings were broken and blood dripped pitifully from its beak. Mungo, now tall and strong, strode angrily towards the culprits.

"What do you think you're doing? Give the robin to me."

It was unfortunate that, just as the smallest boy guiltily put the dead bird into Mungo's hand, Serf emerged from his cell. Mungo would never forget the look of anguish on Serf's face as he took the poor, bedraggled little body between his finger and thumb. His grey eyes looked severely round the ring of frightened faces, but when they came to Mungo their expression changed to bewilderment.

"Mungo, did you do this?" Serf whispered hoarsely.

Unable to believe that Serf could even ask such a question, Mungo was struck dumb. In the momentary silence, the other boys exchanged sly glances. How delightful if Mungo, of all people, should be blamed!

"It was Mungo, Father."

"Yes! I saw him too. He grabbed the robin off the roof and broke its wings."

"He was trying to pull its legs off."

"And bite off its head."

"He said he was going to eat it for supper, Father."

The absurdity of these accusations brought Serf to his senses.

"I'm sorry, Mungo," he said sadly. "Of course I know it wasn't you."

The pain on his old friend's face cut Mungo to the quick. At the same instant, he felt power tingling in his hands once more.

"Give the robin to me, Father," he said.

Very gently, Mungo laid the dead bird on the palm of his left hand. With his right forefinger he stroked its head, then smoothed its injured wings. With a tiny shudder the robin blinked, then opened its eyes wide.

"Fly to Father," encouraged Mungo.

The robin staggered onto its feet and cocked its little head. It flew straight from Mungo's palm onto Serf's shoulder. While the schoolboys goggled, it pecked cheekily at his ear.

Which was a happy ending, in a way. But this time Serf refused to listen to Mungo's pleas for mercy for the other pupils.

"First they killed my bird, then they lied and tried to set me against you," he said. "Why should I spare such villains yet again?"

Mungo sat in his cell, pressing his hands over his ears to shut out the sound of young boys howling. This is the last straw, he said to himself. I can't stand any more. I've got to get away from here and make a fresh start somewhere else.

But Mungo's heart sank as he imagined the pain of explaining his decision to Theneu, and to Serf.

5. Crossing the River

"Of course you must go, if that's how you feel." Theneu sat across the hearthstone from Mungo in her leaky little hut, observing him with calm blue eyes. In some ways the years had been unkind to Theneu; at thirty-three her fair hair was streaked with grey and her face lined from harsh weather and hard work. Yet the woman who had once been a princess wouldn't have changed her draughty hut for a queen's palace. She had found peace in the little community at Cuilen Ros, the respect of her neighbours and the love of her son. But Theneu didn't have a possessive nature; she had always known that one day Mungo would go. "If God is telling you to leave, you have no choice. When you explain, Father Serf will understand," she said.

Mungo felt deeply relieved. As he had walked along the shore, feeling his new monk's habit long and heavy against his bare legs, he'd been afraid that his mother would feel rejected and let down. But he still felt uneasy.

"I just hope God really is telling me to go," he said, "and that it isn't only me wanting to escape. For ten years I've been bullied and made a fool of, and I haven't hit back because you and Father Serf taught me that ours is a God of peace. But I've wanted to punch noses and, since that business with the robin, I've wanted to do worse than that. I really hoped the taunting would stop when I became a monk, but nothing's changed. How can I serve the God of love if I hate the people I live with?"

"You can't," said Theneu firmly. "Look at it this way. If your years at school had been happy, by now you'd be so attached to the place that you wouldn't want to leave. As it is, you've never really put down roots, which suggests that God always meant you to move on."

Mungo was grateful for her support. But when Theneu asked, "When are you going to tell Father Serf?" he twiddled his rope belt and looked at the floor.

"I'm not sure. Maybe in a day or two," he muttered, then changed the subject. "What'll you do when I'm gone?" he asked.

Theneu shrugged her thin shoulders.

"What I've always done," she said. "Gut fish, take my turn at the loom, say my prayers. Until the time is right for me."

"What time?"

Theneu laughed.

"You aren't the only one with plans," she said teasingly. "I haven't given up my dream of being a nun. Of course I shan't leave Cuilen Ros while Father Serf is alive. But one day I'm going to found a convent, and you're going to help me."

They sat for a long time in companionable silence. Only when the cracks of daylight in the thatch darkened, Mungo said he would have to go. Theneu walked with him between the rows of huts, drawing her thin cloak close against the chill of the late autumn afternoon. On the water's edge they embraced wordlessly and Mungo moved away. Suddenly he turned back.

"Mother, who was my father?" he asked abruptly.

He had never asked before, and Theneu had been thankful. Now she shivered as she looked at Mungo's tanned face, with its large nose and wide, good-tempered lips. His bright fair hair curled thickly around his monk's tonsure, the shaved patch on the crown of his head. Thank God, she thought fervently, that he bore no resemblance to that figure of her nightmares, Prince Owain of Cumbria, with his greasy black hair, close-set eyes and small, moist mouth.

"He was a prince and he was a bad man," she said at last. "Be glad that you're not like him, my son."

What Mungo hadn't felt able to tell Theneu was that he planned to run away. When Serf had laid his hands on Mungo's head and ordained him as a monk, Mungo had promised to obey Serf. There would be a big problem if he asked permission to leave, only to have Serf refuse. Better just to take off, Mungo thought, and hope to be forgiven afterwards. On a deeper level, he dreaded witnessing Serf's grief at their parting. It was unlikely, he knew, that they would ever see each other again.

So Mungo prepared in secret. As the leaves drifted down and another year crept towards winter, he saved bread and apples from his meagre meals. Silently he said goodbye to the monastery cows and horses, to Serf's robin and to the sea birds that skimmed the mud-flats of the Gwerid. He would slip away just before daybreak on Sunday morning, he decided, while Serf and the other monks were still in their cells. Only it wasn't to be as easy as that.

Dawn was still a metallic streak on the eastern sky when Mungo crept cautiously from his cell. He would be travelling light; all he had was a leather bag containing food and his precious psalm-book, and an ash wood stick which he had trimmed for himself. Pulling his hood over his head, Mungo moved lightly over the frosted yard to the gate. Easing up the bar, he slipped out into the lane that ran along the river bank.

So far, so good. Quickly, in almost total darkness, Mungo loped to the point where the familiar lane became a muddy, overgrown track. There wet grass slowed his pace; hindered by the long skirt of his habit he blundered along, swiping impatiently at the grass with his stick. He was desperate to put distance between himself and the monastery before the bell rang for morning service in the church.

Mungo knew that he must go inland, to find a place where he could cross the river. In the strengthening light the dark water rolled sullenly; on the other side of the track was rough moorland studded with copses of undernourished trees. Ochel, the range of hills where Mungo had tramped with Serf on summer days, was hidden behind a pall of mist. But the path improved, and ahead of him Mungo could see the great estuary narrowing sharply. God willing, he thought, he would find either a ford or a ferry before nightfall.

Oppressed by the dreariness of the landscape, Mungo began to sing:

> *The Lord is my protector;*
> *He is my strong fortress...*
> *He defends me like a shield;*
> *He protects me and keeps me safe.*

The familiar words comforted him and helped him to stop imagining the scene at Cuilen Ros, where by now Father Serf must know that the son he loved had run away without even saying goodbye. Mungo knew that if he thought about that his resolve might fail him. The day could end with his return to the monastery to throw himself at Serf's feet and ask forgiveness. Which would only mean, he reminded himself firmly, that the pain of parting would have to be endured again, another time.

It was about midday, Mungo reckoned, when he began to feel hungry. By then the Gwerid had tapered and a long, low island had appeared in midstream. With the wind singing in the tall reeds and the river licking its muddy lips the place was eerie. Mungo thought he'd be glad to be clear of it.

As he sat on his cloak on the damp grass, eating dry bread and a bruised apple, Mungo studied the island. Could he wade over to it, he wondered, then to the opposite shore? It was impossible to guess how deep the water was, but the tide was ebbing and he could swim. He had almost made up his mind to try when he heard a rustling in the tall reeds behind him. Grabbing his stick, he whipped round in alarm — but could see no one.

It must have been a bird, thought Mungo, trying to laugh. During the morning he'd seen geese and a heron, balancing on one leg in the shallows. All the same he repacked his bag in a hurry. He was tying the thongs when he heard the rustling again. This time it was sharper and — Mungo gasped in horror — accompanied by an all too familiar cough. Mungo froze on his knees as the reeds parted and Serf, bent and breathless with exertion, stumbled towards him over the squelchy ground. Mungo's eyes popped with astonishment. The idea of Serf's chasing after him had never entered his mind.

It would have been easier, of course, if Serf had stamped and shouted, or even been huffy and reproachful. What made the meeting so terrible was that Serf seemed to have lost all his normal strength and dignity. It was as though now Mungo was the grown-up and Serf the child. The old man collapsed on the cold grass with tears running down his furrowed cheeks.

"Mungo, don't go! Please, my son, don't leave me," he cried.

When Mungo edged over and put his arm round the heaving shoulders, Serf leant against him, sobbing openly. By this time Mungo was weeping too.

"Father," he choked, "I'm so sorry. I ran away to spare you this ..." He faltered, knowing that this was barely half the truth. He had really wanted to spare himself. With a great effort, Mungo pulled himself together. "Dear Father, I have to go," he explained. "Because of me, my brother monks are torn apart with envy and spite. We both know that they can only learn to be good if I'm not there."

"Then let me come with you," begged Serf childishly, but Mungo shook his head.

"You don't really want that, Father," he said. "You'd miss Cuilen Ros and your dear green hills far more than you'll miss me. Besides, what would your people do without you?" When Serf didn't answer, Mungo went on gently, "I must find my own path from now on. But I'll never stop loving you and praying for you. And I'll be depending on you to pray for me."

Still Serf said nothing. As the dismal day began to fade into early night, he and Mungo sat with their arms around each other, father and son for the last time. Mungo dreaded saying, "I have to go now," and cruelly leaving Serf to find his own way home. At least he was spared that distress. Along the river bank two figures appeared, hurrying through the chilly dusk. As they drew near, Mungo recognized them.

"Look," he said kindly. "Here come Brother Caef and Brother Rhyn to escort you home."

As the monks approached, Mungo helped Serf to rise. The storm of the old man's grief had abated and his last words to Mungo were practical ones.

"When you've crossed the river, keep going westward

until you come to a village called Kernach. There you'll find an old friend of mine called Fergus. He'll feed you and give you advice about the next stage of your journey."

"But what if I can't find him? Suppose I lose my way?"

Suddenly Mungo was the child again. A faint smile flickered on Serf's lips.

"You said you wanted to find your own path," he pointed out. "You'll have to trust God to lead you on it."

Mungo took his friend in his arms and hugged him fiercely, but he couldn't say the word "Goodbye." Leaving Serf to greet Caef and Rhyn, he plunged down the bank into the grey water. A moment later he was running headlong across the marshy island, jumping from one tussock to another with his bag bouncing at his side. Then he was in the river again.

Mungo had reached the far bank when he realized two very strange things. He had travelled half a mile in the time it took to say a prayer. And for all that the tide was rising and the water running swift and dark, he was scarcely wet at all. As he plodded away into the dusk, Mungo knew how Moses must have felt when God divided the Red Sea, so that his chosen people could safely cross.

6. Finding Fergus

That night, as darkness came, Mungo crawled into a cleft between two overhanging rocks. He had slept in the open before, but always on summer nights with Father Serf lying nearby. Mungo had lain curled up in his blanket cloak, watching the stars appear in a bluebell sky. He had listened to the chuckling of water and the confident voice of the old man saying his prayers.

> O stars of heaven, bless the Lord,
> Praise him and make him great forever.
> O nights and days, bless the Lord...

Now it was a less kindly season. For the first time in his life, Mungo was on his own. But as he lay on the cold ground, feeling the creeping damp and smelling the smoky scent of decaying leaves, he wasn't afraid. Surely, he thought, God's help at the river was a sign that he'd taken the right decision. And although the parting from Serf had been heartbreaking, at least it was now over.

Mungo slept soundly. When he awoke, he found that the weather had changed. It was a clear blue morning, with dew glistening on the grass like millions of tiny pearls. Mungo couldn't help feeling optimistic as he shook out his cloak and splashed the sleep from his eyes at a nearby stream. He would have an apple for breakfast, he decided, and keep the rest of his bread for the middle of the day.

Taking his bearings from the rising sun, Mungo picked up his bag and turned his face to the west.

For a while, Mungo could see Serf's hills billowing behind a blue veil. He passed the foot of the highest rock he had ever seen, with a wooden-walled fortress clinging to its crest. Beyond that was wild moorland, made dangerous by pools hidden among bristling rushes. The sun was sinking and vapour coiling above the heather when, after a hard day's journey, Mungo reached a huddle of thatched huts in the lee of unfamiliar hills.

"Excuse me. Is this place called Kernach?" he asked a young man who was herding geese into a pen for the night.

The young man shook his brown head.

"Kernach's further west," he said. "Half a day's journey, perhaps." He must have seen Mungo's tired disappointment, because he added kindly, "You can come home with me, if you like. We've broth and some bread, and you're welcome to bed down, if you don't mind being squashed a bit."

"Oh, yes, thank you," said Mungo delightedly, as he followed the stranger towards his hut. "What's your name?"

"I'm Wynt," was the reply, "and here's my brother, Clynog."

That night, with a good meal of turnip and mutton broth inside him, Mungo talked to Wynt and Clynog over the peat fire. Eagerly he told them about his God, and the peace he offered to those who believed in him.

"He fills the hungry with good food," he assured them, "and sends the rich away with empty hands."

The two young men were moved by Mungo's eloquence. But when Mungo offered to baptize them, they shook their heads, glancing at each other with nervous brown eyes.

"We need time to think," said Wynt, "about such an

important decision."

Mungo hid his disappointment, reminding himself that it would be the first of many.

"I'll try to visit you again," he said. "My God and I are grateful for your kindness."

In the morning, Wynt showed Mungo the path towards Kernach.

"Keep the hills on your right. Towards noon you'll see a loch with a little wood on its shore. Kernach is beyond the wood."

So Mungo set out again, thankful for a dry cloak and the cold meat which Clynog had insisted on putting in his travelling bag. The watery sun was at its zenith when he saw a small loch filling a moorland hollow. Mungo ate Clynog's food on its shore, then hurried on into the wood. He was anxious to find Fergus's house before nightfall.

Kernach was a bigger settlement than any Mungo had seen before. It had many huts and was surrounded by strips of cultivated land. Smoke hovered overhead like a fawn cloud as reek from the fires rose through gaps in the thatch.

"Do you know where I can find Fergus?" Mungo asked a woman who was hurrying home with a basket over her arm.

She looked at him rather indignantly.

"Of course I can," she said. "This is a Christian town and Father Fergus is our priest. Though not for much longer," she added in a softer, sadder tone.

"What do you mean?" asked Mungo uneasily.

"Father Fergus is dying," sighed the woman. "If you have business with him, you'd best be quick about it."

Fergus's house stood on the fringe of the little town, beside a wooden church which reminded Mungo achingly of the one at Cuilen Ros. Nervously he knocked, and after a moment heard shuffling steps within. The door opened a crack and an elderly woman's face, bound in a white headcloth, peeped out.

What happened next astonished Mungo. Instead of saying, "Yes? What do you want?" the old woman uttered a loud exclamation of relief. Throwing the door open she grasped Mungo by the front of his habit and almost dragged him over the threshold. "Thank God," she said devoutly. "I began to think you would never come."

"You were expecting me?" Mungo gasped.

"Father Fergus was," the old woman replied.

Peering through the usual smoke-haze, Mungo made out some simple furniture. There were stools, a shelf containing beakers and wooden plates and a cauldron hanging on a chain over the central fire. On one side, on a straw mattress, a frail, aged body was propped up with a pillow. As Mungo approached, milky blue eyes opened in a thin, white-bearded face. A smile of astonishing radiance lit up Fergus's ravaged features.

"Open the gates, for the Lord is with us," he whispered. "Now God will let his servant leave in peace."

Mungo knew the words, but he had no idea what Fergus meant.

"Have you really been expecting me, Father?" he asked, kneeling down and taking the old man's hot, eager hand in his.

"Oh, yes." Fergus nodded quite vigorously. "I've been begging God to let me die because I'm in great pain. But again and again I've heard a voice in the dark, telling me to wait for Kentigern. That's you, isn't it?"

"Yes," said Mungo, although his baptismal name sounded strange to him. "Abbot Serf calls me Mungo," he added.

"You come from Abbot Serf?" Fergus laughed in

delight. "Then I am blessed indeed." He rested for a few moments, then went on, "Listen, Mungo. My last task on earth is to tell you what God wants you to do. In the morning, you must place my body on the cart which you'll find behind my house. Nearby you'll see two white bulls, which you must harness to the cart. Don't try to guide them, but let them pull the cart wherever they choose. Where they stop, God wants you to bury my body and build a church."

They were the strangest instructions imaginable, but Mungo couldn't question someone so obviously alight with the Holy Spirit.

"I shall do as you say, Father," he promised, making the sign of the Cross over the old man's head.

Fergus slept peacefully after that, with Mungo sitting beside him. Gratefully Mungo ate the food which the old woman brought him, then he got down on his knees again and prayed. Towards dawn, Fergus died.

The white bulls made no made no protest as Mungo harnessed them and yoked them to the cart where Fergus's body lay under a white cloth. The townsfolk stood in huddles in the thin morning light, their breath vaporizing on the frosty air. Some wept openly, but no one tried to stop Mungo as, with a handful of hay, he coaxed the bulls onto the courtyard before the church.

For a moment the animals hesitated, pawing the ground and lifting their horned heads to sniff the wind. They set off so suddenly that Mungo was caught unawares. Rushing after the cart, he only just managed to swing himself up onto the shaft. He hung on for dear life as the unreined animals thundered away towards the west.

7. King Rhydderch's Warning

Whenever he tried, later in life, to describe the journey with the white bulls, Mungo was lost for words. It was like trying to recreate a dream; he had an impression of travelling faster than a shooting star, rushing headlong through darkness and light while the moon sang and the wind screamed and the earth went spinning like a silver coin on the edge of chaos. Mungo saw sun and stars, mountains and burning deserts. He felt spray on his cheeks and heard the shouting of the sea.

Mungo had no idea how long the journey had actually taken. But when the bulls finally slowed and halted, his first thought was prosaic — and terrible. Suppose that, in such a wild flight, Fergus's body had fallen off the cart? With reeling head and thumping heart, Mungo scrambled back and turned down the cloth. He needn't have worried. Fergus lay peacefully in the morning sunshine with his white hands folded on his breast. His eyes were closed and there was a smile on his lips, as if he knew a wonderful secret. Mungo sighed with relief. As he loosed the bulls, however, he was frowning perplexedly. He knew that he had to bury Fergus's body — but how? He didn't even have a spade.

Just for a moment, though, Mungo was too tired to fret. Sitting down on the grass beside a burn, he looked around him with appreciative eyes. The bulls had stopped in a lovely glen, one side of which was faced with shiny grey rock. On the other a grassy slope descended from a little birch wood to the burn, which tumbled and chattered as it scurried away to join a much larger river. From his elevated position, Mungo could see the river, sleek and silver under the soft winter sky. Smoke rising above its bank suggested houses sheltered by trees.

Mungo was trying to summon energy to go and look when, on the rocky side of the glen, he saw a young man with a fishing rod and a string of fish. He was jumping sure-footedly among the boulders at the water's edge, and when he saw Mungo he shouted a greeting.

"Hello, Brother! Need any help?"

"I do, indeed. Thanks," Mungo called back.

"I'll come over."

Two more nimble leaps, and the newcomer was on Mungo's side.

"I'm Telleyr," he said, grinning widely.

"Mungo," said Mungo, clasping the outstretched hand. "Can you lend me a spade? I've got to bury someone."

Just for an instant, Telleyr's mouth and eyes went circular with incredulity. Then, because they couldn't help it, the two young men burst out laughing. Mungo didn't think Fergus would mind. As they walked down the side of the stream to the village, Mungo explained as well as he could what had happened.

"I didn't choose to come," he said. "The bulls did — guided by God, I'm sure. Now I have to bury Fergus."

Telleyr nodded. He didn't seem surprised.

"It was a good choice," he said. "Most of the people in our village are Christians — I am myself. Long ago, our ancestors were converted by a man called Bishop Ninian. There's a tradition that he blessed the piece of ground where I found you as a Christian cemetery, but no one was ever buried there. We have our own cemetery close to the village, and naturally people like to be buried with their families."

"But that's wonderful," said Mungo in amazement. "It means I can bury Fergus in holy ground."

"We," corrected Telleyr. "I'll get my brother Anguen to help."

It was hard work digging a grave in the cold winter earth, but the three young men toiled side by side in growing friendship. In the late afternoon, when the sun was sinking behind distant mountains, they wrapped Fergus's body in the white woollen cloth and gently buried him. Mungo, as he lashed two branches together to make a cross for the grave, thanked God for bringing Fergus to such a beautiful resting place.

I'll keep the cart and the bulls, he thought, as he prepared to accompany Telleyr and Anguen back to their parents' house. They'll be useful when I build my monastery. But strangely, when he went to tether them, the bulls had disappeared.

"Who does the land round here belong to?" asked Mungo next morning as he helped Telleyr to gut fish — a skill he had acquired as a child on the bank of the Gwerid. He had spent the night as the guest of Telleyr's family and was anxious to be helpful.

"To King Rhydderch Hael," Telleyr replied. Mungo knew that "hael" meant "generous," so this sounded promising.

"Where does he live?" he asked eagerly.

"At Alclut, further down the river," said Telleyr, gesturing vaguely. "Why?"

"I'll have to get his permission to build my monastery by the burn where we buried Fergus," explained Mungo. "Do you happen to know the king at all?"

Telleyr's look was scathing.

"Brother Mungo," he said, tossing a silver-scaled fish into a leather bucket, "people like me don't know people like him. Nor do people like you," he added crushingly.

Telleyr's tone brought a flush to Mungo's cheeks. He was opening his mouth to say, "My father was a prince, actually," when he remembered the truth about his father. A prince and a bad man, Theneu had said. Not someone to boast about, ever.

So it was humbly, with nothing to offer in return, that Mungo walked ten miles down the river Clut to the fortress of King Rhydderch Hael. He could see it from far off, perched on a towering rock, pushing up its ugly wooden head into the sky. It took Mungo an hour to scale the narrow path cut into the cliff face, dizzy and afraid to look down at the seagulls wheeling like a snowstorm above the black water. But everything was going well for him at present. He found it quite easy to persuade the guard at the gate to take him to the king.

King Rhydderch, a youngish man with red hair and a bushy beard, was sitting by the fire in a room little larger than a cell. It was so draughty that the fire guttered and little dust balls scuttled across the floor like living things. Mungo, who had never seen a king before, had imagined Rhydderch in a sumptuous robe and a golden crown. Whereas, although the cloth was finer, Rhydderch's simple tunic and leggings weren't much different from Telleyr's.

"You're welcome, Brother Mungo," said King Rhydderch, when Mungo had rather awkwardly bowed and given his name. He pointed to a stool and, when Mungo had seated himself, added pleasantly, "What can I do for you?"

Mungo was delighted by the king's lack of ceremony.

Eagerly he poured out his story, telling Rhydderch about Theneu and Serf, about Fergus and the extraordinary journey with the bulls.

"Fergus was a holy man, my lord King," he concluded. "I trusted him when he told me to build my monastery where the bulls stopped. But I can't, of course, unless you let me."

He looked hopefully at Rhydderch, who had been watching him keenly. The king stretched, changing his position in his chair.

"Brother Mungo," he said, "I like you and you may build your monastery where you wish. But I must warn you, there's a snag."

"A snag?"

Mungo, who had been ready almost to jump for joy, looked questioningly at the king. Rhydderch explained.

"I am King of the Britons of Alclut," he said. "My kingdom stretches fifty miles to the north and hundreds of miles to the south. Of course I have overall control, but I can't be everywhere at once. So the country's divided into sections, each with an overlord who owes me loyalty. The land around Cathures is governed by Prince Morken — a competent man, but he isn't a Christian and he doesn't particularly like Christians." Rhydderch looked uncomfortable. "What I'm saying is ..."

"I know what you're saying, sir," said Mungo. "I shouldn't expect any favours from Prince Morken. I'll try to keep out of his way."

"Then go ahead, with my blessing," Rhydderch said. Mungo thanked him with shining eyes. The king couldn't help smiling at his boyish enthusiasm. "I'll ride over one day and see how you're getting on," he promised.

Mungo flushed with pleasure. He stood up, bowed and walked backwards to the door, hoping that he wouldn't fall over his long habit. He was almost outside when he stopped suddenly and said, "My lord King!"

"Yes?"

"Did you say that the glen where I'm to live is called Cathures?"

"The village is," replied Rhydderch. "The burn's called the Mellendonor. I don't think the glen has a name."

"May I give it one?" asked Mungo. The king nodded. "Then I'll call it Glasgu,the dear green place.'"

8. The Dear Green Place

Mungo had never been so happy in his life. Sitting by the racing burn in the mild, springlike weather, he planned his monastery in his mind's eye. I'll build my own cell beside the great rock, he thought, where I can hear river sounds and watch the dippers building their nests beside the waterfall. I'll have a guest-house on the opposite bank, and when other monks come to join me they can build their cells further down the glen. The mill will have to be by the burn, of course, and we'll need a barn and shelters for our cows and sheep. Mungo didn't worry about where his fellow monks, or indeed his cows and sheep, were to come from. He was confident that God would give him companions and the means to live.

The first priority was to build his own cell. He knew how, because he'd helped to build cells at Cuilen Ros. With tools borrowed from Telleyr and Anguen's father, he cut branches from the languid willows which dropped over the burn. When he'd hammered in a small circle of stakes and soaked the branches to make them pliable, he wove the willows in and out of the stakes to make a rounded, basket-like wall. With the help of Anguen and Telleyr, Mungo fetched mud in leather buckets from the bank of the Clut. The three young men got hilariously filthy plastering the woven wall to keep out the wind and wet. When he'd made the framework for the roof, however, Mungo stood scratching his head.

"I need straw for the thatch," he said, "but I don't know where to find any."

"You can use turf," Anguen told him. "It keeps out the rain better and it's less likely to blow away in a gale."

So off they went to cut turf from the grassland behind the wood. They brought it back on Fergus's cart, now with Telleyr and Mungo pulling it.

At the end of a week, Mungo was ready to move into his new abode. Anguen and Telleyr's father, Kedic, had made him a stool and a little shelf to keep his psalm-book off the damp floor. Their mother, Bera, had given him a clay lamp and a jar of oil. On his last night in her house, she also offered Mungo a sheepskin.

"You'll be so cold up there," she said anxiously, "with only your cloak to keep you warm."

Although he was grateful, Mungo refused firmly.

"I've found a long stone to sleep on and another for my pillow," he explained. "My cloak will cover me well enough. Don't look so horrified, Bera," he added, smiling. "Didn't Jesus Christ choose to be poor and to live a hard, uncomfortable life on earth? I'll only feel close to God if I try to live the same way. Besides," he laughed, "I don't intend to do much sleeping. My old abbot, Serf, was up most of the night, praying and chanting psalms in the dark. I mean to do the same."

Bera sighed and shook her head, but Telleyr and Anguen nudged each other excitedly.

"You ask him," urged Anguen.

"No, you," whispered Telleyr.

Eventually they blurted it out together.

"We want to be monks too."

Of course, it wasn't so simple. Next day, as they squatted on the floor of his cell, Mungo spelt out to his friends just what their choice would mean.

"I've lived a monk's life since I was seven, and it isn't easy," he told them bluntly. "You'll always be poor and often cold and hungry. You'll never be able to marry and have children. And you'll have to obey orders, which you may not like, since I'll be handing them out. On the other hand," Mungo smiled at their solemn faces, "God will be your friend and you'll have the hope of everlasting life when you die. Are you still keen?"

"Yes. Very," was the reply.

"Great," Mungo said. The two brothers were crawling out under his sackcloth door-curtain when he added, "Hang on. There's just one other thing. You'll have to learn to read and write."

There were gasps of horror as Telleyr and Anguen backed into the cell again. Their dark eyes were popping with alarm.

"What on earth for?" demanded Anguen.

"So that you can read the Gospels and the Psalms," explained Mungo patiently. "Later on, I'm going to have a writing-room where we can copy the Scriptures and make books."

"But who's going to teach us?" quavered Telleyr.

"Me, I suppose," Mungo said. "At least, until someone comes along who'll do it better."

He hoped fervently that someone would come along soon. I can't spend all day teaching, he thought, not with so many other things to do. Still, when he looked out from his cell a few days later, and saw the two identical cells which Anguen and Telleyr had built further down the glen, Mungo knew that God was answering his prayers.

The first words he taught his friends to read were: *The Lord is my shepherd. I shall want for nothing.*

In the weeks that followed, the words were proved true. As Mungo became known in the district as a young man with a sympathetic ear and a healing touch, gifts of affection and gratitude were shyly offered.

"Some cloth from the village loom, Brother, to make new habits for you and your friends."

"I netted a big salmon last night, Brother. Thought you'd enjoy a slice."

"I've been baking today. Would you like a fresh loaf?"

There were larger gifts, too. When King Rhydderch rode over to visit Mungo, he made him a present of a strip of land. Later he sent bags of seed corn, a cow, three pregnant ewes and an iron bell.

"Someone in my family brought it from Rome, I think," Rhydderch told Mungo, next time they met. "It's of no use to me, so you may as well have it."

Mungo was delighted to have a bell from Rome. He would be long dead before the story began to circulate that he'd gone to the Eternal City himself and brought it back as a souvenir.

As the snow melted on the mountain peaks beyond the Clut and primroses opened in crevices of the grey rock, recruits began to arrive at the monastery. There was Nidan, who had been educated by monks in Drumalban, and who was happy to take over Mungo's teaching duties. There was Conval, who had crossed the sea from Ireland and, hearing of Mungo from a fellow traveller, had eagerly travelled up river to Glasgu. To Mungo's delight, Conval was an ordained priest. This meant that he could celebrate Mass and give Communion to others, as Mungo couldn't, yet.

"We'll build our own church," said Mungo, smiling at

grey-eyed, red-headed Conval. "How good of God to send you to us!"

Yet of the score of men, mostly young, who gathered in Mungo's glen that spring, none were more welcome than two bedraggled creatures who turned up one evening in a downpour, exhausted and soaked to the skin.

"Don't you remember us, Brother?" asked one, peering anxiously at Mungo's slightly puzzled face. "Wynt's the name," he added, wiping his streaming cheeks with his sleeve.

"Wynt! Of course I remember," cried Mungo. "You gave me shelter on my way to Kernach. And you're — Clynog?"

Sensing another question, Clynog answered.

"We told you we needed time to think. Now we've thought. We want to be baptized and join your family. Or should I say household?" he asked, peering through the plashing rain at the cluster of turf-roofed cells and the half-finished wooden church standing in a quagmire.

"It's both, really," said Mungo, putting an arm round Wynt and clapping Clynog on the shoulder. "The family's mine and the household's God's."

Now days began to melt quickly into months and months into years. Under King Rhydderch's protection, Mungo's monastery grew and flourished. Mungo was ordained priest and, at the early age of twenty-five, was made a bishop, in charge of all church matters in Rhydderch's kingdom.

One summer evening, Mungo sat in the doorway of his cell, looking down the glen to which the white bulls had brought him nine years before. All his plans were accomplished. The church with its tidily thatched roof and wooden cross, the guest-house, the kitchen and dining-room, the writing-room, mill and byre all stood as he had envisaged them. The green sward at the foot of the glen was crowded with cells. Monks, in the white habits Mungo had chosen for them, went quietly about their work. As Mungo sat listening to the birds chirruping and the burn scampering over its softly coloured stones, his "dear green place" really seemed like Paradise. Yet as there was a snake in Paradise, so there was a shadow in Mungo's domain. The shadow was Prince Morken.

9. Prince Morken's Barns

Prince Morken. Mungo knew King Rhydderch's deputy by sight, a hunched, hollow-cheeked man whose hard mouth and glittering eyes hinted at a dark, cruel nature. Black-haired, black-suited and riding a black horse, Morken aimed to inspire terror, and he did. The people of Cathures cowered when he rode through their village, lashing out with his whip at anyone who got in his way. He was known for random acts of violence; a young man flogged, a farm set on fire, a dog trussed up and drowned. Morken called it "reminding the scum who's in charge," but everyone knew he arranged these happenings because he enjoyed them. Mungo had always found the prince an uncomfortable neighbour, but had never really felt threatened by him.

"We have King Rhydderch's permission to be here," he reminded his uneasy companions. "Provided that we don't antagonize Prince Morken, he won't move against us. I promised the king I'd keep out of his way. Now I'm ordering you all to do the same."

Which had worked well enough for a long time. If he met Prince Morken, Mungo greeted him with a smile and a sign of the Cross. Morken responded with a sneer. Then, within a month, two things happened.

One was that Mungo became a bishop. The other was that Morken appointed as his second-in-command a man called Cathen. It soon became clear that from now on Morken would plan outrages. Cathen would carry them out.

Trouble at the monastery began on a spring morning when two of Mungo's followers, returning from the village, were pelted with mud and stones. The young men responsible were riding with Cathen.

"Look at the mess we're in, Father," wailed the monks, running to Mungo with mud and tears streaming down their faces.

Mungo couldn't hide his irritation.

"Pull yourselves together," he said testily. "If you can't cope with a bit of mud-throwing, what on earth will you do if something really bad happens to you?"

The mud-throwing, however, was the prelude to more sinister incidents. Cattle belonging to the monastery sickened and Brother Wynt, who was in charge of the livestock, reported to Mungo that he thought they'd been poisoned. Sheep were stolen and dead rats thrown over the monastery gate. Worst of all in September, when the monks' corn had been cut and stored for the coming winter, one night the barn caught fire.

Because there was little water in the burn and the river Clut was half a mile away, the building couldn't be saved. The monks were forced to watch in horror as their barn and its contents became a vast bonfire. It was Brother Anguen who later spoke sombrely to Mungo.

"I see Prince Morken's hand in this, Father. According to my father, Kedic, it's common knowledge that Morken's furious about you becoming a bishop. He thinks ..." — Anguen shuffled awkwardly — "that you're too big for your boots these days. And with King Rhydderch away until the spring ..."

"You're not supposed to gossip with your father, Anguen," Mungo reminded his friend. "You know the rule,Only talk about important matters.' Now, haven't you any work to do?"

But his tone was mild, for Anguen meant well and he was only confirming what Mungo already knew. What Mungo didn't foresee was that soon he would be forced to ask Prince Morken for help.

The winter was hard that year. Before Christmas, snow came spinning out of the north, turning the monks' cells to igloos and clinging like sheep's wool to the monastery fence. Pinched and shivering, the monks limped about their work on chilblained feet. In the church hacking coughs drowned the singing of the Psalms.

A week into the new year, a sudden thaw made the Mellendonor burst its banks. Cells were flooded. Men and beasts floundered in the mud. Worst of all, there wasn't enough to eat. No corn meant no bread, and although the villagers tried to help, they had barely enough for themselves. By February, when frost again bit deep, Mungo realized that his fifty monks were close to starvation. Many were too weak to work. The oldest and frailest began to die. Since King Rhydderch was absent, Mungo decided that he would have to appeal to Prince Morken.

The sky was leaden and there was snow in the offing as Mungo set out for Prince Morken's stronghold on the bank of the Clut. The river was the colour of slate and even the grass was as grey as Mungo's mood. He wasn't a proud man, but he hated having to ask a favour from someone who despised God and abused his creatures. As he drew close to Morken's scowling fortress with its rings of barbed fences, Mungo prayed fervently: *O God, stay close to me. My strength, be quick to help me.* Taking a deep breath, he knocked on the door with his bishop's staff. The guard who admitted him smirked openly.

"Bishop Mungo! What a surprise!" Morken didn't bother to rise from the couch where he was lolling by the fire, gnawing a chicken leg. Throwing the remains to his wolfhound, he wiped his greasy mouth with his sleeve. "Do tell me," he drawled. "Is this a social call?"

The room smelt of sweat, dog's excrement and stale food. Mungo felt disgust, but knew he mustn't let it show. Ignoring Morken's provocative tone, he spoke simply.

"My lord, I need your help. Perhaps you heard that last autumn our barn was destroyed by fire. As a result my monks are starving, and three have died. Please, give us some corn from your own store to see us through until spring."

Even as he was speaking, Mungo knew what the response would be. Morken's mouth tightened and his small eyes flickered in the firelight.

"You have a nerve," he snarled. "You've been squatting on my land for years without permission, hiding behind that fool Rhydderch's cloak-tail. And now you dare to come crawling to me, because your dismal, good-for-nothing crew is starving! Who cares? I hope you all die."

Somehow, Mungo kept his temper. I'll try again, he thought. Just one more time.

"Prince Morken," he said. "You have barns by the river overflowing with corn — far more than your household can possibly need. All I ask is that you share, as I would if our positions were reversed."

Morken spat, perilously close to Mungo's feet.

"If our positions were reversed, Bishop," he said contemptuously, "I would die of shame." Seeing Mungo's cheeks redden, he grinned triumphantly. "I'll tell you what," he mocked. "If you can persuade your God to move all the corn in my barns to your place without anybody else touching it, I'll not only give you the corn. I'll become

a Christian!" This thought seemed to tickle him so much that he almost choked laughing. Then suddenly he looked vicious again. "Get out," he snapped, "before I set my dog on you."

On his way back to the monastery in the bitter afternoon, Mungo paused on a little rise overlooking the Clut. Quietly he spoke to God. "You know, Lord," he said, "that I never ask you to do anything that I can do by my own efforts. But I can't get the better of Prince Morken, or feed my monks, without your help. Please, Lord, confound that wicked man. Give us our daily bread."

There was a pause of perhaps a minute, although to Mungo it seemed much longer. Then suddenly, a rush of wind blew back his hood. Thunder growled overhead and fork lightning tore the sky. Wide-eyed and terrified, Mungo saw the Clut heave and bubble, as if all its water was coming to the boil. As he fell on his knees a towering, white-crested wave came crashing ashore. Ripping three of Prince Morken's thatched barns from their foundations, it tossed them like coracles into the tide.

Somehow Mungo managed to scramble to his feet. Hitching up his robe, he ran panting towards the junction of the Clut and the Mellendonor. All the inhabitants of Cathures were on the bank, goggling open-mouthed as the floating barns rounded the corner. A gasp went up as they beached themselves neatly on the grass outside the monastery fence. At once the wind dropped. The river rippled like dark silk.

10. A Dreadful Encounter

That night, kneeling on the damp floor of his cell, Mungo thanked God sincerely for the astounding miracle he had performed. Later, however, when he was lying on his bed of stone, he acknowledged ruefully that his troubles weren't over. For every person who saw the power of God in the shifting of the barns, there would be another who accused Mungo of sorcery, of using spells to steal Prince Morken's corn. Two things were certain. Prince Morken would break his promise to become a Christian. And he would not take his humiliation lying down.

"We'll keep the corn," Mungo told his monks in the church next morning, "because God has given it to us. But I must warn you that there are bad days ahead. In the Scriptures we read how Christ's followers were persecuted by their enemies. Sometimes they were even put to death. I hope that won't happen to us, but our faith will certainly be put to the test."

There was silence as the monks glanced fearfully at each other in the flickering lamplight. When Mungo had blessed them, they filed out soberly into the rain.

Prince Morken's reign of terror began almost immediately, since Cathen had recruited every ruffian in the district. Monks out visiting the sick were ambushed and beaten. Cattle-raiding and sheep-stealing became daily occurrences. Burning torches were hurled over the fence and drums beaten constantly when the brothers were trying to sleep. Four monks left because they couldn't take any more. Another died, apparently of fright.

Prevented from hitting back by Christ's instruction to love one's enemies, Mungo confined himself to praying for God's help. This time, however, God didn't seem to be in a hurry. On the morning when his dear friend Wynt came home dazed and bleeding from a bad head wound, Mungo knew he must do something himself.

"Clynog and Anguen, look after Brother Wynt," he said grimly. "Telleyr, come along with me. We're going to call on Prince Morken."

Telleyr looked aghast, but he knew better than to argue. He had to scamper to keep up with Mungo as, once again, the bishop strode towards the tyrant's stronghold.

This time Mungo didn't find Morken alone. Lounging in a corner of the dirty room was the rascally Cathen. Mungo, who had heard a rumour that Morken was scared of his lieutenant, thought he'd never seen a meaner, crueller, more insolent face than Cathen's. In comparison, Morken's weaselly features seemed merely peevish. While Cathen drew a dagger from his belt and fingered it, Telleyr did his best to look dignified by the door. Mungo faced Morken across the littered floor.

"What do you want now?" demanded Morken, who was once more sprawling on a couch. "Are you going to do another magic trick and bring my corn back?"

He grinned at Cathen, who winked encouragingly.

"My monks have restored your barns," replied Mungo evenly. "We kept the corn at your own suggestion. In view of the violence we've been suffering, I've come to ask what became of your promise to become a Christian."

Morken stared, then tittered incredulously. Behind him, Cathen made a rude noise.

"Prince Morken? Become a Christian?" he sneered. "That'll be the day."

"I wasn't speaking to you," Mungo said.

The dagger left Cathen's hand with the speed of a striking snake. Whistling past Mungo's head, it impaled itself in the wall a hair's breadth from Telleyr's ear. Telleyr cried out. He couldn't help it. Cathen roared with laughter.

"Go on then," he incited Morken. "What are you waiting for? Give the Christian a good kick for his impudence. Or do you need me to do it for you?"

Morken leapt to his feet. His face was twisted with fury at Cathen's insolent tone. For an instant, he seemed undecided who to kick. But he was afraid of Cathen, and he knew that Mungo saw his fear. Baring his teeth, he ran at Mungo, aiming a vicious kick at his kneecap. Knocked off balance, Mungo staggered and fell backwards. Cathen howled with glee.

"Push off, monk," he chortled, as Telleyr breathlessly helped Mungo to his feet. "Run and tell God what bad boys we've been and ask him to punish us. I reckon we'll wait a long time."

"Not very long, I think," Mungo replied.

There were those who would say it was coincidence, but Mungo didn't think so. Neither did Telleyr. Next morning, when the monks were at breakfast, Kedic arrived white-faced at the dining-room door. Mungo saw him gesticulating and went out, closing the door behind him.

"What's the matter? Is Bera all right?" he asked anxiously.

Kedic nodded, licking his lips.

"She's well. I came to tell you that Cathen, Prince Morken's deputy, has had an accident."

Mungo looked less surprised than Kedic had expected.

"What happened?"

Kedic shrugged.

"They say that he and Prince Morken spent the whole of yesterday drinking," he said. "Seems they thought they had something to celebrate. It was almost dark when Cathen left. No one knows exactly what happened, but the alarm was raised when his horse came home riderless. Cathen was found dead at daybreak, his neck broken by his fall."

A few days passed before Kedic, who knew everything, brought another piece of news to the monastery. Prince Morken was ill with fever and a terrible swelling in his feet. According to Kedic, he was roaring with pain and the magicians attending him were unable to help. This didn't surprise Mungo very much either.

On an early spring morning, when the glen was full of bird calls and rushing water, word came that the tyrant was dead. Relief flooded the countryside, but Mungo grieved for two wasted lives.

11. Terrible News

"What a wonderful place this is. I can't ever thank you enough for letting me settle here." Mungo smiled at his friend King Rhydderch, who was strolling with him on the bank of the Mellendonor on a clear June evening. Rhydderch nodded vaguely. He had arrived at the monastery earlier and had stayed to supper, though he'd eaten little and obviously had something on his mind. Unusually, during their evening walk, Mungo was having to do all the talking. "If only my mother's wish to be here could be granted, I'd have no prayers left unanswered," he said.

"Is old Serf still alive, then?" asked Rhydderch, making an effort to look interested.

"Very much so," laughed Mungo. "He's well over eighty, but I hear he still goes on expeditions into the hills, wearing out monks half his age. My mother's adamant she won't leave Cuilen Ros until he dies," he added wistfully, for time was passing and helping Theneu to found a convent at Glasgu had become one of Mungo's most cherished ambitions.

Suddenly King Rhydderch plucked a flower from the bank and violently tore it to pieces.

"Don't pray for your mother to come here, Mungo," he said harshly. "When you hear what I have to tell you, you'll thank God she's miles away. We must speak privately," he added urgently, with a fearful glance over his shoulder.

Mungo was shocked. He had never seen strong, confident King Rhydderch in such a state.

"In here," he said, stepping aside among the trees. Quickly he led the king to a little clearing where monks had been cutting wood. "You can say what you like," he assured Rhydderch. "No one will overhear us."

The king sat down with his back to a tree, as if he needed something solid behind him. Mungo sat on a sawn-off tree stump. Licking his lips nervously, Rhydderch began.

"Did you know that Prince Morken had cousins?" Mungo shook his head. "A couple of black-hearted villains," said Rhydderch bitterly, "named Hueil and Caw. When Morken died last year, Hueil came to Alclut and asked me to appoint him ruler instead. Seemed to think it was his right as Morken's next of kin."

"What did you say?" asked Mungo uneasily.

"I told him to take his squinty-eyed rascal of a brother and get off my land," replied Rhydderch, with a spurt of his old spirit. "Then I kicked him downstairs."

"I see. And did they get off your land?"

"Yes," said Rhydderch, "cursing and threatening what they'd do to me, and to you for killing their cousin with evil spells. My spies followed them down river, then lost them in the mountains of Dal Riata. I must say they covered their tracks brilliantly. No matter how I tried, I couldn't get any news of them. Until now."

"Now?"

"The rats have reappeared," groaned Rhydderch. "It seems they've spent the last year recruiting every ruffian and malcontent between Alclut and Pictland. They've camped with an enormous army at the end of the old Roman wall. My spies tell me they'll attack within two days."

Rhydderch's voice cracked with despair. Mungo was appalled.

"But — you'll fight back, won't you?" he asked.

His heart sank when Rhydderch shook his head.

"I can't, Mungo," he said. "Hueil and Caw are wealthy and can bribe people to fight for them. Two-thirds of those I trusted have gone over to their side. I don't have the men or the money."

"But what about my church? My monastery?" cried Mungo. "You're the king. Will you let innocent men be murdered?"

Rhydderch flushed at Mungo's reproach, but he kept his temper.

"If I do fight," he said patiently, "then your monks will surely die. But Hueil and Caw aren't interested in your monastery. They want you and me. I intend to slip away into the mountains with a few friends and wait for Hueil's new supporters to get tired of him. I suggest you do the same. Even vipers like Hueil and Caw aren't going to lay waste the land they want to rule."

Mungo leant forward and put his head in his hands.

"But where shall I go?" he whispered.

Mungo's dejection seemed to rouse Rhydderch from his. Getting to his feet, he brushed the dead leaves briskly off his tunic.

"Go south," he said decisively, "by Caer Luel into the Cumbrian mountains. Then move westward into the land of Cymru. King Cathwollon Liu is a friend of mine, and there's an abbot, Dewi, who'll shelter you. If the situation here improves, I'll send you word."

Rhydderch didn't wait to say goodbye. When Mungo raised his head, the king was gone.

Mungo never slept much, but that night he didn't sleep at all. In the midsummer half-darkness he prowled the woods above the monastery, hearing through grief the mournful night voices of fox, bittern and owl. Always, in the past, he'd seen the next step on his life's road clearly. Now, his mind was in turmoil.

Should he take Rhydderch's advice and slip away from Glasgu before his enemies came to get him? Should he go to Hueil's camp and give himself up? He would be killed of course, but that wouldn't matter if his death saved other lives. In a frantic moment Mungo even wondered if he should take up arms himself. Surely the people he had converted would come if he called? He had a mad vision of himself riding at the head of a Christian army, slaughtering pagans in Christ's name.

It was revulsion at this sin of thought that brought Mungo to his senses. How could he, a man of God, even think of such a thing? He was on his knees in his cell when the painful answer came to him. Of course, he wanted to protect what he had come to believe was his — his church, his monastery, his people. Only they aren't mine, he thought. They're God's. I must give them back to him.

At three o'clock, when the monks rose for the first service of the day, Mungo as usual led the procession to the church. When the morning hymn had been sung and prayers said, he stood in front of the altar. Tersely he told his brothers what King Rhydderch had told him.

"I'm going to leave you, at least for a while," he said. "Whatever happens, you'll be safer without me. When I'm gone, you must decide for yourselves what to do. I believe that God will protect those who choose to stay, but if you want to leave you may do so."

There was stunned silence. Clynog broke it.

"Do you mean — to come with you, Father?" he asked hopefully.

Disappointment sighed through the church as Mungo shook his head.

"I mean that you're free to go to other monasteries or become hermits in the hills," he said. "I'm the danger. I must go alone."

"I'll stay here," said Nidan firmly, "and trust myself to God."

"And I," said Conval.

"And I."

"And I," said other voices.

"Good." Mungo managed to smile at them. "Nidan and Conval will lead you in my absence. God bless you all."

12. Footsteps in the Fog

It was evening on the second day out from Glasgu when things began to go badly wrong. Until then the weather had stayed fine and Mungo had made progress, although he still could scarcely believe what had happened to him. Sick with disappointment and anxiety about his friends, he trudged along with his cloak slung over his left shoulder. His only other luggage was the leather pouch on his belt and the shepherd's crook which Wynt had proudly carved for him when he became a bishop. At the thought of Wynt, tears welled in Mungo's eyes.

At the beginning, the journey had seemed fairly straightforward. Following the Clut upstream, Mungo had walked on the old Roman road, taking prudent cover only when he saw other travellers ahead. There weren't many; the proud chariots and marching legions of Roman times were long gone. Twenty miles from Glasgu, beyond majestic waterfalls, the great river became a modest stream which trickled away among the heather. On the second day Mungo had again kept to the road, knowing that it would lead him through the hills to Caer Luel, the old garrison town the Romans had called Luguvallium. Once he was there, on the other side of the great barrier wall, he reckoned he would breathe more easily. Then disaster struck.

The road had been almost deserted all day. Mungo, who had had two hours of sleep in three days, was almost dozing on his feet. Suddenly he was jerked awake by the thunder of hooves behind him. Whipping round, he saw a huge horse, ridden by a man in a black cowl, bearing down on him with furious speed. Mungo scarcely had time to leap for the ditch before horse and rider whirled by, tossing up a storm of dust and stones. For a split second Mungo saw the rider's face. With a gasp of horror he thought he recognized — Prince Morken. Only, of course, Prince Morken was dead. A ghost, then, or — God save me, thought Mungo. It's one of the cousins. He's come to get me.

At that moment brave, resourceful Bishop Mungo went to pieces. Without even pausing to consider that if this were true, the rider would surely have stopped, he scrambled out of the ditch and stumbled away from the road. All the pain and loss of the past three days seemed to be jamming his head. The last straw was when he put his hand to his breast and realized that he'd lost the little wooden cross which Father Serf had given him when he became a monk. Sobbing bitterly, Mungo blundered away among the hills.

When the moon rose, Mungo was in a narrow, treeless valley, shivering beside a sullen black burn. The road's too dangerous, I'll have to find my way south by the sun and the stars, he thought wretchedly as he ate a tiny ration of bread and cheese from his pouch. Wrapping himself in his cloak, he lay down and tried to get close to God through prayer. But as night came in that dreary place, Mungo felt that God was far away.

The next day began as badly as possible. During the night the weather had changed and Mungo woke cold, wet and disoriented. With no sun to help him get his bearings, he realized that he must, after all, try to get back to the road. But how was he to find his way among such monotonous, indifferent hills? In the thickening fog he couldn't even see the gap where he'd entered the valley.

Finally Mungo decided to follow the burn. Somewhere it must join a river, and the river might run by a road. He had been squelching along for an hour when he stopped suddenly, raising his head like a deer sniffing the wind. Terror shook him. Surely he could hear distant voices — and footsteps in the fog.

The rest of that day was the most terrifying Mungo had ever spent. As a boy at Cuilen Ros he had often been afraid, but at least he had seen who was threatening him. Cathen had been menacing, but he had a face. Now Mungo could scarcely move forward for stopping and looking over his shoulder. The harsh squawk of a ptarmigan made him jump with fright. Even the wing-whirr of a lapwing rising from the heather froze his heart. He tried to cry out, "Who's there?" but the fog silently sucked in the words. Was it Caw or was it Hueil, or the ghost of Morken stalking him among these cruel hills?

Eventually Mungo gave up hope of finding a road that day. The cold, unfriendly burn seemed to be going nowhere, yet it was his only guide. When it slithered into a gully between two black rock faces he went with it. Dazed and shivering in his sodden clothes, he limped along, no longer caring much whether he lived or died. When he heard a voice calling, "Father Mungo! Father Mungo!" he thought it was inside his head. When he glanced over his shoulder for the last time and saw a brown-clad, hooded figure hurrying after him, he was almost glad.

"If you're man or devil, do your worst," he cried.

"I'm doing my best," retorted a familiar voice. "Take it easy, Father. It's me, Wynt."

That night, wrapped in a dry, warm cloak, Mungo sat by a camp fire at the entrance to a cave. Aching with fatigue, he watched Wynt grilling trout, while Clynog and Telleyr shook out blankets to make beds in the cave behind. Anguen had gone to fetch water. Presently he came leaping up the hillside carrying two leather bottles, his face split by a bright grin.

"Feeling better, Father?" he asked.

Mungo nodded. Still shaken by his experience and amazed by the sudden appearance of his friends, he didn't yet feel up to asking them just what they thought they were doing. Lightheaded with relief, he could have laughed at them. Dressed in rough brown tunics, they were buzzing around like schoolboys on a picnic, bursting with self-satisfaction. When Wynt, his face scarlet from the fire, passed him a piece of fish on a stick, Mungo ate it ravenously.

"That was delicious," he said.

"Have some more," Wynt replied.

After supper, the friends sat round the glowing embers of the fire. The fog had rolled back, and the hills looked benign under a thin slice of moon. Without prompting, Clynog began to tell the story.

"When we saw you were determined to go alone," he said, "we knew we couldn't stop you. But there was no way we were going to let you go all the way to Cymru on your own, and risk never seeing you again. Before we followed you, however, we reckoned a little preparation was in order — finding extra blankets, you know, and clothes to make us look less like monks."

"You are monks," Mungo couldn't help pointing out.

"No point in advertising it," said Clynog sagely. "This is still Morken's old territory. Anyway, Kedic got us this kit — there's a tunic for you in Anguen's bag, by the way — and off we set, with Brother Nidan's blessing."

"You didn't have my blessing," said Mungo rather tartly.

Now that he was warm and fed, he was perking up again.

"No," put in Telleyr with a grin, "but we didn't disobey you either."

"Convince me."

"You said," Telleyr reminded him, "that we were free to join other monasteries. That's what we're going to do. Join a monastery in Cymru. The same one as you."

The four friends smiled smugly. Mungo couldn't help a snort of amusement.

"Well, tell me more," he said.

Brown-headed Wynt took up the tale.

"We were nearly a day behind you, but we knew there was only one way you could go. Kedic brought us in the cart as far as the Roman road, and we were able to sprint along quickly without long skirts round our legs. Unlike you, Father," Wynt couldn't resist adding slyly.

"Get on with it," Mungo grinned.

"Sure enough, last night we saw you in front of us on the road, but then ..."

"Then a stupid oaf on a horse ran us down," interrupted Telleyr furiously. "We were all thrown into the ditch and skinned our elbows and knees. By the time we'd got ourselves sorted out, you'd disappeared."

"The horseman ran me down too. He reminded me of Prince Morken," admitted Mungo shamefacedly. "I panicked and ran away from the road."

"Ach, these blackbeards all look the same," said Wynt, provoking roars of protest from Anguen and Telleyr, who were both dark.

Mungo looked at them in fond exasperation.

"Tomorrow I'll have to make monks of you rascals again," he warned.

"Oh, yes. Tomorrow," they agreed, laughing.

It was Anguen who finished the story.

"Brother Wynt found your cross in the grass, Father. Otherwise we'd never have known which way you'd gone. It was like a little miracle. We camped in this cave when it got dark, and as soon as it was light Brother Wynt and Brother Telleyr set off to look for you. But the mist had rolled down, and ..."

"It took longer than we expected," said Wynt gently. "Every time we glimpsed you, the mist closed over you again. But never mind. You're safe and we're all together again, Father."

Mungo sat fingering the little cross which Wynt had given back to him. With a full heart he looked round the firelit circle of familiar, affectionate faces. Suddenly he remembered a night long ago, in his cell at Cuilen Ros. He must have been about thirteen, and was having trouble with bullies at school.

"I just want friends," he had wailed, and Father Serf had replied, "You will have friends. But perhaps not here. Not now."

Nor for a long time after, Mungo thought. But the friends he had now had been well worth waiting for.

"I was wrong," he said, "and pig-headed to think I could manage better alone. I'm glad you followed me. Thank you for wanting to come."

13. The White Boar

"Father," said Anguen, as he and Mungo walked together along a desolate shore, "may I ask you a question?"

"You asked a question yesterday," pointed out Mungo. "That was supposed to be your ration for the week."

But he was smiling, so Anguen went ahead anyway.

"I was just wondering — we all were, actually — when we're going to leave this place and build a monastery of our own."

"Why? Don't you like it here?" asked Mungo, sounding genuinely surprised.

"I miss ..." began Anguen, then thought better of it. "Nothing," he said, and they plodded on over the windswept shingle.

What Anguen missed was life on the road. During the months when he'd accompanied Mungo on the long journey into the land of Cymru, he'd come to love the dawns and sunsets, the long tramps among the lakes and blue mountains of Cumbria, the camp fires and sleeping under the stars. He had been proud to be known as a follower of the shining young man who could heal the sick, and whose preaching brought frightened people to trust in the true God. Where Mungo made converts he erected a wooden cross; in his mind's eye Anguen could see a long, triumphant line of these crosses, all the way from Caer Luel to the border of Cymru.

Unfortunately — Anguen thought — the bare-legged, vagabond days had ended all too soon. After weeks of following a wild, rocky coastline, treading springy turf above cliffs that dropped dizzyingly to pounding waves and swirling turquoise pools, Mungo's little band arrived at Mynyw. There, in a hollow above the shore, the famous Abbot Dewi had built his monastery. For Anguen and his friends the carefree time was over.

As Wynt fairly pointed out, on one of the few occasions when he was able to open his mouth without being heard and punished, Dewi was a very holy man. He had Mungo's gifts of preaching and healing, and it was said that the Holy Spirit, in the form of a dove, had once alighted on his shoulder. Unlike Mungo, however, he made no allowances for other people's frailty. While Mungo expected his monks to keep his rules, and regretfully punished those who broke them too often, Dewi was literally a holy terror. A dark, sallow man with glowing eyes, he believed that only by enduring the greatest hardships could a human being get close to God.

Whereas Mungo's rule was, "Only talk about important matters," Dewi's was, "Don't talk at all." Whereas Mungo allowed his monks bread, fish, fruit, and a little cheese, Dewi only allowed his tiny portions of bread and vegetables. His monks had to pray with their arms stretched out in the position of a cross, and stay awake, on their knees, from Friday at dusk until sunrise on Sunday. Immediately on arrival the Glasgu monks had their travelling clothes snatched away from them. As they battled to build their cells in the teeth of an Atlantic gale, their hairy shirts and heavy grey gowns felt like prison uniform.

"You must obey Dewi's rules while we're here," Mungo told them firmly. "Later on, when I've found a suitable place, we'll have a monastery of our own."

Which was hopeful, except that days and weeks went by without the matter ever being mentioned again. To the Glasgu monks' unease, Mungo and Dewi got on tremendously well. They were constantly together, walking, consulting, reading, praying. Twice they went off for several days, leaving Brother Adrian, a zealous Irish disciple of Dewi's, in charge.

"I hope old Dewi isn't giving Father Mungo ideas," muttered Clynog to Anguen, whom he met as he was painfully pulling a cart.

Dewi thought that having horses and oxen made monks lazy. Anguen, weighed down by buckets of water, managed to grin. That night, however, he made up his mind to jog Mungo's memory. The opportunity came next day, when Mungo took him to visit a sick man at a village further along the shore.

"I was going to tell you this evening," said Mungo, "so I may as well tell you now. Dewi's taken me twice to visit King Cadwollon Liu. He's willing to let me build a monastery anywhere I like in Cymru, so we'll be moving on soon."

Anguen, who knew that a show of delight would displease Mungo, nodded solemnly. But he couldn't disguise from himself his longing to be a traveller once again. Nor from Mungo either, apparently.

"You're going to have to settle down again sometime, Anguen," he warned.

"Of course, Father," Anguen replied.

Unlike Anguen, Mungo yearned for a place where he could build a church and a cell of his own. Although he admired Dewi and was grateful for his hospitality, he was tired both of travelling and being a guest. He had been an abbot since he was seventeen years old, and he longed to manage his own affairs again. So, on a sharp spring morning, Mungo was secretly as glad as his companions to fasten on his travelling pouch once more.

"I can't thank you enough for all your help, Father," he said warmly to Dewi, as he picked up his shepherd's crook. "We'll never forget you."

"True," murmured Anguen to himself.

"God bless you all. Go safely and in peace," Dewi replied.

A curtain of fine rain fell across the sun as the little band crested the hill and turned for a last look at the sea. Mungo had decided to go inland, although he still had no clear idea where he wanted to settle.

"Of course I must find somewhere with rich soil, clean water and a good supply of timber for building," he had said to Dewi on the night before he left. "But it must also be a place of God's choosing. When I founded my monastery at Glasgu," he had added, "God provided two wonderful bulls to guide me to the right place."

"I've no doubt God intends to guide you again," Dewi had replied, with one of his rare smiles.

After a month of wandering, however, Mungo was as unsure of God's purpose as when he'd set out from Mynyw. It wasn't that he hadn't seen suitable sites; as he and his companions journeyed through thin sunlight and sweet spring rain, the forests and valleys of Cymru disclosed dozens of perfect places. But however fertile the soil, however sparkling the river, Mungo hesitated then said, "Let's move on." Even Anguen was becoming weary of making and striking camp. Then one morning, when once again the five monks were ready to take to the road, Telleyr suddenly stiffened.

"Look! Over there," he whispered urgently.

Everyone looked. Wynt trembled. Anguen gasped in

alarm. Among the trees, watching them with small, unblinking eyes, was an enormous wild boar. Twice before, during their travels in Cumbria, the monks had encountered such creatures. They had massive shoulders, wicked tusks and evil tempers. Normally they were black. This one was white.

"Careful, everyone," breathed Clynog, tensing himself to spring sideways, dragging Wynt with him, if the boar charged.

The boar didn't charge. It took a few steps forward, pawing the soft forest floor and snuffling with its moist, tender snout. Then it turned and trotted a little way in the other direction. Looking back, it grunted and jerked its shoulder. There was a beseeching expression in its piggy eyes.

"Is it trying to tell us something?" wondered Wynt.

"Of course it is!" Mungo smiled radiantly. "Come with me!"

All day long, with a sense of miracle, Mungo followed the white boar. He was aware of forests, fresh with lacy young leaves, streams running silver through marsh and moorland, slippery defiles and tumbling waterfalls. The boar kept always a little ahead, purposeful and sure-footed, its thick white coat gleaming brightly. From time to time it paused and looked back with a strange, almost human smile. Mungo's companions walked as if in a dream.

At last, towards evening, the white boar stood still on a green bank. The place, where two rivers met, reminded Mungo poignantly of his beloved Clut. To the east were blue-crested mountains. To the north a rainbow trembled on the sky.

"This is the place," said Mungo, going down on his knees to thank God.

While Mungo prayed, the white boar waited respectfully a little way off. As soon as Mungo stood up, however, it trotted meekly forward, grunting and looking up at him with its small, intelligent eyes. The others watched curiously as the creature thrust its snout into Mungo's hand, rubbing against him as tamely and affectionately as a dog. Gently Mungo caressed the boar's bristling mane, fearlessly touching its curling tusks and sharp, pointed teeth.

"God bless you, noble animal," he said. "I wish I could reward you for your help. Since I can't, I pray that God, who cares for birds, beasts and fish, will give you whatever is best for you."

The boar appeared content. As Mungo made the sign of the Cross it bowed its head graciously in return. Without looking back it trotted away, vanishing for ever among the trees.

14. An Angry King

In the golden summer that followed the departure of the white boar, more than the scenery reminded Mungo of his "dear green place." Everything that happened at the meeting of the Elwy and the Clwyd — even the name sounded a bit like "Clut" — seemed to be a replay of events at Glasgu long ago. While the five monks were busy building their cells, kindly villagers brought gifts of fruit and bread. King Cadwollon Liu contributed oxen and a plough, sheep, cows and corn.

Meanwhile, men of every age began to arrive, all eager to join Mungo's community. Some, already monks, had been sent by the abbots of neighbouring monasteries to give the newcomers a hand. Some had been hermits living in isolated caves around the coast, but now wanted to join the household of God for a while. Others were converts to Christianity, bright with new belief and avid to serve God.

Fortunately, everyone could understand everyone else. The kingdom of Alclut, Cumbria and Cymru were all inhabited by Britons, who spoke the same language. Mungo welcomed them all and made them feel at home.

"It isn't easy to be brave and trusting all the time," he said. "I know what it's like to be terrified and feel that God is far away. But if you pray and try to keep my rules, God will be pleased and so shall I."

Mungo's kindness was infectious. The new monastery was a happy place where people weren't afraid to smile.

All through the summer months Llanelwy, the "holy

place by the Elwy," was a building site. It was so chaotic that sometimes Mungo wished he was a hermit. From the door of his cell he watched monks toiling, their sleeves rolled up and their long skirts hitched through their belts to free their legs.

Newcomers were building their own cells. Other monks were clearing and levelling the site for the church. Some were chopping down trees while others stripped them, cut them and fitted them together to make walls for the church, kitchen and barn. Even if they were only "talking about important matters," the air was full of voices, rising above the sounds of chopping, banging and hammering.

I'll be glad when winter comes, thought Mungo, then felt guilty because really everything was going so well. Or so it seemed until, one early September afternoon, a scowling stranger came riding out of the forest. He had a band of heavily armed soldiers at his heels.

"In the name of Beli," he roared, "who are you and what in thunder do you think you're doing on my land?"

At the name of Beli, the pagan god of the Underworld, the monks froze in horror. Dropping their tools, they huddled together, watching the intruders warily. Mungo, who had been helping to thatch the church, climbed down the ladder and walked over to the dark figure on a restless black horse. Again his sense of uncanny repetition was strong. The intruder reminded him of Prince Morken, who still appeared to Mungo in nightmares from time to time. God, help me, he prayed, but had no time for more. Slithering from the horse's back, the stranger stamped towards him.

"I asked you a question," he hollered. "Who are you? Are you in charge of this rabble?"

"My name is Kentigern," said Mungo, using his formal

name. In a moment of passing amusement, he thought it unlikely that this pop-eyed ogre would ever call him "dear friend." "I have King Cadwollon Liu's permission to build a monastery here. I didn't know I also needed yours — whoever you are."

For an instant, Mungo thought the man was going to explode. His face turned purple and his body seemed to swell inside his tunic.

"Whoever I am?" he spluttered. "I'm Maelgwyn Gwynedd, king of the north, that's who. This land belongs to me ..."

"Under King Cadwollon Liu, I believe," interrupted Mungo, the truth dawning on him. Of course, Maelgwyn Gwynedd must be Cadwollon Liu's underling, just as Morken had been Rhydderch's. Only Cadwollon Liu had forgotten to warn him.

"Am I right?" he inquired.

Maelgwyn's eyes narrowed.

"Cadwollon Liu is far away," he rasped. "You have until this time tomorrow to dismantle this rubbish-heap and get your good-for-nothing tramps off my land. I'll be back to see that you've obeyed me," he added, shaking his fist in Mungo's face.

Out of the blue, Mungo had a chilly premonition.

"You'll be back," he agreed quietly, "but as for seeing ..."

Just for a second, Maelgwyn looked into Mungo's eyes. Something he saw there silenced him. Vaulting onto his horse, he galloped away under the trees. A moment later, a terrible scream tore the air.

"I'm scared, Father," confessed Wynt that evening. He and Mungo were walking round by moonlight, making sure that all the animals were safely penned for the night. "I think something awful happened in the wood today."

Mungo looked at Wynt's kindly face, gaunt and shadowed in the greenish light. The only thing that had really upset him during his encounter with Maelgwyn Gwynedd was hearing men like Wynt called "good-for-nothing tramps."

"Yes," he agreed calmly. "I think so too. But you don't have to worry. Whatever happened was God's business."

"Do you think the king will come back?" asked Wynt.

"Oh, yes. He'll certainly come back."

"And we shouldn't be — you know — getting ready to leave?"

Mungo laughed.

"What do you think?" he said.

Even so, it was an anxious time. On Mungo's instructions, work on the monastery continued next day as usual. But everyone was subdued, and as noon passed tension was palpable.

"I knew we should've put up the fence first," muttered Clynog.

"A fat lot of use that would've been," growled Telleyr.

"Do you think Father Mungo knows what's going to happen?" asked Asaph, a very young monk who was helping with the thatch.

"You never can tell with him," Clynog replied.

In fact, Mungo didn't know what was going to happen, although he had a fair idea of what had occurred in the wood. What he had known, the instant when he and Maelgwyn Gwynedd had looked into each other's eyes, was that the angry king was a deeply unhappy man. He might swear by Beli, but that dark god didn't comfort him.

The sun was casting long tree-shadows on the grass when Maelgwyn Gwynedd again came out of the wood. But how differently from yesterday! Now Mungo's monks gasped with horror and pity as they watched the king, supported by two white-faced boys, groping blindly towards them.

"It's all right, Father. Hold onto us. We're nearly there," said one of the youngsters kindly as Maelgwyn stumbled, reaching out and clawing at the air.

Quickly Mungo went to him. Avoiding the boys' indignant looks, he took Maelgwyn by the hand.

"I'm here," he said. "Come and talk to me."

No one moved as Mungo put his arm round the king's sagging shoulders and guided him away among the trees.

It was cool under the leaves. Mungo helped Maelgwyn to sit down on the bank of a stream, then sat beside him.

"When did this happen?" he asked, gazing at the king's now sightless eyes.

"Yesterday, just after I left you," replied Maelgwyn sadly. "My guards wanted to return and kill you, but I was so terrified I just wanted to get home. I was afraid to come back, but my wife said I must and my boys said they would come with me." There was a pause, then Maelgwyn went on fearfully, "Your God's done this to me, hasn't he? To punish me for threatening you?"

"Not exactly." Mungo could have wept with pity for this sad, confused man whose family loved him. "My God isn't cruel. He just wants you to understand that he's greater than your god, and that he loves and protects those who trust him. That could be you, too. Would you like me to tell you more?"

Maelgwyn nodded.

"If I believe, will your God let me see again?" he asked pathetically.

"He will let you see again anyway," promised Mungo, touching Maelgwyn's flickering eyelids with his right hand.

15. Asaph's Miracle

Of course, the story of King Maelgwyn's blinding and his cure went round the district like wildfire. At first people found it hard to believe that their irascible, stingy overlord had really turned into a just and generous ruler, but gradually they accepted that he had. Freed from terror of the dark gods, Maelgwyn and his family were baptized by Mungo in the river Clwyd. Before the last red leaves had fallen from the trees, most of those who lived on the king's land had followed his example.

Maelgwyn's spectacular conversion did Mungo and his friends nothing but good. Gifts and offers of help flowed in. Soon the fence was raised, enclosing the church and other communal buildings. Here too the monks who had come before the king's conversion were allowed to have their cells. Outside the fence were the mill and the cattle sheds, and a whole village of cells built by more recent arrivals. Then there was the school.

Mungo had never wanted to be a schoolmaster. He'd really had enough of schools when he was a pupil at Cuilen Ros. But the two kings to whom he owed so much, Cadwollon Liu and Maelgwyn Gwynedd, were determined to have their sons educated at Llanelwy. So, within eighteen months of his arrival, Mungo had a school on the other side of the river. Slightly bemused, he watched little boys playing football and hide-and-seek. He got cross, just as Serf had done, when their noise disturbed his reading.

"You'll have to be firm," he told Anguen, whom he'd put in charge. "Don't have favourites, and send any bullies to me."

Don't have favourites. It was an unwritten rule of Mungo's and it was troubling him. This was because, for the first time, he knew he was in danger of breaking it.

Mungo had never wanted any life but the one he had. Sometimes, seeing a happy couple together, he'd thought marriage would be pleasant, but he'd always been far too busy to fret over what he didn't have. Only now, when he saw fathers fetching their boys at holiday time or watched King Maelgwyn having fun with his two sons, he felt unexpected pain. It was ironic, really. A hundred men, aged fifteen to seventy, called him "Father," yet he could never have a real son. Around the same time, Mungo began to notice Asaph.

No one could deny that Asaph was special. Already well educated, he had come from a nearby village only days after Mungo arrived at Llanelwy.

"How old are you?" Mungo had asked, smiling at the bright, eager young face.

"Thirteen."

"Can you read and write?"

"Of course."

"What else can you do?"

"Anything, with God's help."

It was soon apparent that this was true. Asaph could build a fence and thatch a byre. He could write letters in Latin and knew the Psalms by heart. He could milk a cow and cook — and, like Mungo himself, he had healing hands.

All of this might have been a bit much for the other

monks to take, had not Asaph been such a friendly, modest lad. He had a blue-eyed, merry face, and his goodness wasn't the kind that showed other people up. Mungo saw no reason to hold him back, and at the age of sixteen he was ordained priest. No one would have blamed Mungo for being proud of Asaph, but Mungo didn't delude himself. Asaph was his favourite, his substitute son. I'm making the same mistake that Serf made with me, he thought bitterly. God deliver me. I know what I'm doing is wrong.

For a while, however, God didn't interfere. Even when the building was completed, Mungo was busy; there were visits to make, letters to write, people to care for. Mungo needed a secretary. Asaph got the job.

If anyone had asked Mungo, he would have said he expected to die at Llanelwy. As the years passed, he remembered his monastery at Glasgu and prayed for the safety of his friends there, but he stopped thinking of going back. That he might be confusing his own wishes with God's will never entered his mind.

It was the worst winter anyone could remember. Snow came early, whirling from a yellow sky. It changed the contours of the landscape, iced the thatch and lent mysterious beauty to the trees. After the second snowfall cells disappeared completely and tunnels had to be dug between them and the church. Next came frost, hardening the snowy world into what came to seem permanence. Day after day the sun skulked below the horizon. By night the stars glittered like fragments of ice.

Mungo was used to the cold, and inclined to impatience if any of his monks complained. After Christmas, however, it became hard for him to ignore the number who were ill with colds and fever. Even harder to ignore was the fact that, for the first time in his life, Mungo was ill himself. His head ached and he could scarcely breathe. Asaph found him in the church one afternoon, shivering violently.

"You must go to bed, Father, or you'll die," said Asaph sternly, and it was proof of how bad Mungo felt that he agreed.

While Mungo crept to his cell, Asaph ran to fetch his own cloak and blanket.

"You need a little fire in here, Father," he said, as he covered Mungo in the vain hope of getting him warm.

"I'm all right," Mungo tried to say through chattering teeth, but Asaph had gone.

What happened next would have astounded Mungo, had he not thought it was a delusion caused by his high temperature. Only days later, when he had recovered and Brother Hoidel, the cook, asked to speak to him, did he learn the truth.

"I feel so bad, Father," confessed the elderly monk, his lined face pale with remembered fear. "I only meant to tease the lad. It would have been my fault if he'd been badly burned."

Mungo was startled.

"What do you mean?" he asked.

"Brother Asaph came into the kitchen as I was making broth," Hoidel replied. "He said,'I need some burning wood to warm Father Mungo,' and I said,'Have you brought something to carry it in?' He said he hadn't, and I said, just meaning a joke,'You'll have to carry it in your tunic, then, won't you?' Of course I meant to fetch him a pan, but before I could put down my ladle ..." — Hoidel's faded brown eyes widened — "down went the lad on his knees and with his bare hands, Father ..."

"So it was real," said Mungo, his eyes widening too.

"Father?"

"Asaph arrived in my cell carrying two blazing logs in his tunic," Mungo explained. "At the time, I thought I was dreaming." He shook his head perplexedly, then patted the old monk on the shoulder. "Stop worrying, Brother Hoidel. No one can prevent miracles," he said.

16. Going Home

Mungo believed in miracles. He'd performed them often enough, with God's help. In the past, though, he'd always seen a reason why God would interfere in the natural way of things: to take away pain, to comfort the broken-hearted, to prove his love and power. The miracle of the burning logs, however, made Mungo uneasy. At first it seemed pointless, and dangerously like a magic trick. It took time for Mungo to grasp the important point, that it was Asaph's miracle, not his. Then light began to dawn.

As usual, in no time at all everyone for miles around had heard about the miracle. Others besides Hoidel had seen the young man with fire in his arms. As the last tatters of snow melted, Mungo noticed how the other monks' attitude to Asaph had changed. Friendliness was now tempered with respect, even awe. Despite his youth, Asaph's advice was sought, his opinion heeded. The miracle, Mungo realized, was Asaph's stamp of authority. He's the man of the future, thought Mungo. He'll be abbot here when I'm gone. He felt guilty about the strength of his fatherly pride.

Still, for all his fondness of Asaph, Mungo wasn't in a hurry to relinquish his post. He always felt vigorous as spring approached, and as soon as the snow was gone he began to make plans. This year he wanted to build overspill monasteries on the coast, and hoped to find time for a visit to Dewi in the autumn. But God had other plans for Mungo. Asaph's miracle had been timed precisely.

It was a watery spring afternoon as Mungo walked home alone from King Maelgwyn's house on the other side of the wood. He was glad of the exercise. The trouble with kings, he found, was that they ate too much and got huffy if you didn't do the same. So to be polite you ate meat and puddings and all sorts of rich food your stomach wasn't used to — and had indigestion afterwards.

Otherwise, it had been a happy meeting. King Maelgwyn had given Mungo land for the new monasteries and was now offering oxen, ploughs and sheep. As Mungo walked home, listening to the gurgle of swollen streams and the twitter of birds in the newly green branches, he felt that life was good. The monastery came in sight, its thatched roofs rising in peaks above the neat wooden fence. I love this place, Mungo thought. I'm so glad God brought me here.

At this moment of great contentment, Mungo saw Asaph hurrying along the path towards him. It was obvious from his tense expression that something was afoot.

"What is it, Asaph?"

"A messenger has come, Father, from the north. Says it's urgent. I've asked him to wait in the church."

Mungo nodded. If the words "from the north" caused a nervous fluttering in his chest, he didn't let it show. Passing Asaph, he hurried on towards the gate.

The messenger came out of the shadows as Mungo entered the church. In the frail starlight of the sanctuary lamp, Mungo peered into a keen, weatherbeaten face. The young man was haggard with sleepless travel, his hair dusty and his cloak stained.

"Are you Bishop Kentigern?" he asked respectfully.

"I am. Your name?

"Coel, my lord. I've come from King Rhydderch Hael ..." — Mungo started at the name — "to tell you that he has overcome his enemies in battle at Arfderyyd, near Caer Luel. Hueil and Caw are dead, so it's safe for you to return to Glasgu. King Rhydderch begs you to come."

There was a moment's silence, in which Coel waited for a response he didn't get. He coughed, looking vaguely embarrassed.

"Have you eaten?" asked Mungo. Coel shook his head. "We have a guest-house. I'll send a brother to wait on you," Mungo said.

He turned away abruptly, hoping that Coel hadn't noticed his pique and disappointment.

I suppose I'll have to go, Mungo thought dismally that night, as he knelt in his cell listening to the soft pattering of spring rain. I know that God has already chosen Asaph to succeed me, and no doubt this is his way of delivering me from the folly of pretending that Asaph's my son. But it was difficult to be grateful just then. As he climbed onto his uncomfortable bed, Mungo could feel only the bitterness of parting, the weariness of starting all over again.

"The news from Glasgu isn't good, my lord," Coel had said when Mungo visited him in the guest-house before evening prayers. "The monks you left behind had to leave when Hueil came to power, and a lot of the people you converted were too frightened to go on being Christians. King Rhydderch wants you to know there's much to be done."

Only with difficulty had Mungo stopped himself from saying, "Then let him get someone else. I can't be bothered. I'm too old."

Eventually, only half an hour before the bell rang for

morning service, Mungo fell asleep. He woke feeling half dead, and dreading having to break the news of his departure — especially to Asaph.

Strangely, in the end, it was Asaph's reaction which made everything else tolerable. On the river bank, where Mungo had taken him for privacy, Asaph took the news of his promotion with quiet confidence.

"I suppose I knew the day I picked up the burning logs that God had chosen me for something special," he said thoughtfully. "I've been trying to prepare myself — not that I expected anything to happen quite so soon. You will pray for me, won't you, Father?"

The young man spoke modestly, but his words were like a knife in Mungo's heart. Asaph doesn't care a bit that I'm leaving, he thought. For a dreadful moment Mungo wanted to lash out bitterly, accusing Asaph of ingratitude and lack of love. What stopped him was a sudden, guilty memory of his own hard-heartedness when he'd walked out on Serf long ago. Why blame Asaph for having a similar sense of his own destiny? Why blame him for not needing an earthly father when he had God? It was Mungo who was at fault, for wanting something he'd always known he couldn't have. Alone in his cell at bed time, Mungo couldn't help shedding a few tears, for Serf and for himself. But when morning broke, he felt as free as a bird.

No one else took the news of Mungo's leaving as calmly as Asaph had. The monks wept and the schoolboys howled. Even King Maelgwyn couldn't hold back his tears. Only Telleyr, Anguen, Clynog and Wynt were happy. When they heard that they were to accompany Mungo back to Glasgu, joy and relief were written on their faces.

"We were afraid you might decide to leave us behind,"

admitted Clynog. "Now that we're getting old — well, middle-aged, you know."

"You speak for yourself," snorted Telleyr.

"Out on the road again," grinned Anguen. "Just like old times, Father."

"It's good to be going home," said Wynt.

17. A Royal Welcome

It was a warm, still evening in June. Midges danced in clouds and the harebells were intensely blue. Mungo and his friends sat on a sandy bank in their undershirts, bathing their swollen feet in an icy burn. Behind them, their damp habits were spread out on the grass to dry.

"How long till we reach Glasgu, d'you reckon, Father?" asked Wynt, as he shared out bread and cheese provided by a kind cottager from whom they'd asked directions.

The leaving of Llanelwy had been exhausting emotionally and, as usual in early summer, they'd journeyed either in ferocious heat or through chilly, windswept rain. Wynt's private ambition was to build himself a cell at Glasgu and never leave it again. Mungo scratched his midge bites and considered.

"Four days," he said. "Maybe three, if we don't fall into any more bogs."

Everyone laughed, though it hadn't seemed funny at the time. With the blue mountains of Cumbria retreating through haze, the monks had spent many hours tramping along the southern side of a great river estuary. Even in sunshine it was an eerie firth, by turns sluggish and mercurial, with sandbanks visible beneath the crawling water. It had been a relief when the hoarse cries of sea birds faded and they'd come at last to a place where it seemed possible to cross.

"Sulwath," the woman who'd fed them had called it.

They ought to have been warned, since the name meant "muddy ford." But they'd pressed ahead, and soon going back would have been as difficult as going forward. For what seemed eternity they had floundered under the pitiless sun, stepping on tussocks which slid treacherously, pitching them into stagnant pools and seams of black, treacly mud. Black flies buzzed horribly and Clynog had been frightened by a snake. Twice Mungo had had to pull Anguen out of the squelch with his crook, and at one point he'd thought they'd have to carry Wynt. It had been a colossal relief eventually to reach firm ground.

"We'll have to stop now," Mungo had said, looking ruefully at his mud-encrusted friends, "get cleaned up and rest overnight. We can't go on the road looking like this," he added. "Suppose we met someone important!"

It was meant as a joke, though later it would seem prophetic.

Very early next morning, when the sun was drawing yellow lines on the eastern sky, the monks rose and put on their clean though travel-stained habits. When they'd said their prayers and tied on their sandals, Mungo began to lead them north-west through the heather.

"Perhaps we'll see the Clut today," said Wynt hopefully.

Now they were back in the country Mungo remembered so vividly, a landscape of rounded hills, sooty moorland and dark, winding rivers. Hawks hovered and small beasts scuttled, but there was never a house nor a human being in sight. Towards noon the monks came upon a dusty track, half hidden by bramble and gorse.

"I think this will lead us to the Roman road," Mungo said.

Just then they heard it — a long, unbirdlike whistle, carried on the upland breeze. The monks tensed, exchanging nervous glances. Another whistle answered as, to their horrified surprise, a bright red head reared out of the heather. Instinctively Mungo's fingers tightened on his crook.

"We've nothing to steal!" he shouted. "Please, let us pass!"

Alarm was misplaced, however. When the owner of the red head stood up, he was plainly unarmed. He signalled, but not to them. Then something wonderful happened. All of a sudden the air was full of voices, happy, laughing, unthreatening. Heads popped up everywhere, like flowers. Running and skipping down the track came men, women and children, waving and calling out.

"Hooray! Here's Bishop Mungo!"

"Hello, Father! It's been a long time."

"Welcome, Brothers! It's great to have you back."

Speechless with amazement, Mungo and his companions watched the people jostling excitedly as they formed two lines, one on either side of the path. Between the lines came someone vaguely familiar, dressed in a purple tunic and with a gold circlet on his head. It was the grey hair and beard that briefly fazed Mungo, but then ...

"King Rhydderch!" he cried joyfully, and the next moment the two old friends were hugging and thumping each other on the back.

"This is amazing!" gasped Mungo. "But how on earth did you know where to find us?"

"Easy," laughed Rhydderch. "Maelgwyn Gwynedd sent riders to tell me you were on your way, and I've had spies out ever since. We — Father Nidan and I — decided you deserved a welcoming party. So here we are."

"Nidan?" Mungo felt his knees trembling. "Is Nidan here?"

"I'm here, Father."

A tall, white-robed monk with a lined face and greying hair came forward and knelt for Mungo's blessing. Wynt burst into happy tears. Then the lines broke and everyone came surging forward, eager to speak to Mungo and his friends. Mungo greeted other monks from Glasgu, old friends from Cathures, warriors who had been faithful to King Rhydderch Hael.

"Do you remember me, Father? I'm Indeg the swineherd."

"Please, Bishop, bless my baby. Math's his name."

"I'm Arthgal, the king's bodyguard. We've been years on the run, Father, but now we can all go home."

The king waited good-humouredly until he could get a word in, then he said, "We're camped at Hodelm, a few miles off. Shall we walk ahead, Mungo?"

So Mungo and Rhydderch walked together, as they'd done so often long ago. As the sun was westering they came to a green meadow fringed with trees, above a tranquil river. A great wooden cross had been erected on an adjacent hill. In the meadow there was a village of improvised huts and tents. The smoke of many camp fires rose serenely into the blue evening air.

"Nearly time for supper," said Rhydderch, clapping his hands and licking his lips.

While the five monks bathed and said prayers together, a great feast was laid out on the grass in front of Rhydderch's tent. There were mounds of fresh bread and platters heaped with meat and grilled trout. There were baskets of fruit, whole cheeses and puddings made with honey and thick, rich cream. Clynog, Anguen and Telleyr stared open-mouthed. They had never seen such a banquet in their lives. Wynt, bewildered by the variety of cooking smells, looked faintly sick.

"Do we have to eat everything, Father?" he whispered in dismay.

"Just do your best," advised Mungo, who knew how he felt. "We'll all have stomach-ache, but at least we shan't have offended the king."

18. The Old Woman at the Gate

"It's good to be going home," Wynt had said at Llanelwy. Mungo hadn't argued, but he hadn't really known what Wynt meant. Monks weren't supposed to have homes, only the hope of heaven when they died. Not until he'd come to the Sulwath, and had seen wild green hills crowding the tall, opalescent sky, had Mungo understood how Wynt felt. He too was a man of the north, and yes — it had felt like going home.

Back in Glasgu at last, that feeling had remained. Relief was in the air, joy that the pagan rule of Hueil and Caw was over, and that Christian King Rhydderch had triumphed. At the monastery, Mungo was surprised how little had changed. Despite the monks' long absence, the walls of their buildings still stood, and there were many willing hands to help with re-thatching them. The bell from Rome, which Nidan had hidden before he left, was rehung. Once again its sweet voice rang out over the Clut, calling people to prayer.

Of course there were changes too. Old friends had died, among them Kedic, who was deeply mourned. Father Conval, who had spent the years of Mungo's absence keeping the Gospel alive at Rhynfrwd, further down the Clut, asked permission to build his own church there. Father Nidan set out on a long journey into Pictland, from which he would never return. But former brothers came back and new ones arrived. Within a year the monastery was thriving once again.

Although he loved his cell by the grey rock, Mungo did-n't have much time to spend there. He was always busy, travelling round the countryside, preaching the Gospel and healing the sick. It was true that many former Christians had renounced their faith in fear of Hueil and Caw; it need-ed patience and understanding to bring them back to God. Mungo felt he was succeeding, and only one thing clouded his happiness. He was worried about his mother.

Twice, since he got back from Cymru, Mungo had sent messages with travellers who said they would be passing Cuilen Ros. Unfortunately, he had no way of knowing whether the messages had been delivered, and he had had no reply. Serf, Mungo thought, must certainly now be dead; the old abbot had been over eighty when Mungo fled from Glasgu more than ten years ago. So what had happened to Theneu? Was she still at Cuilen Ros? Had she come to Glasgu and, finding Mungo gone, assumed that he was dead? If so, where was she now? I must go to Cuilen Ros and ask for news of her, thought Mungo anx-iously. But all through spring and summer he was too busy to go away.

It was a sharp, smoky summer evening in September when Mungo, sitting in the doorway of his cell, saw Wynt hurrying up the glen. Wynt had a scurrying gait when he was bothered, and he was scurrying now. Rather reluc-tantly, Mungo turned his eyes away from the misty river and the setting sun.

"What's the matter, Brother?" he asked, getting up from his stool.

Wynt looked embarrassed.

"I'm very sorry to trouble you, Father," he said, "but there's a problem."

"Go on."

"Well," continued Wynt, shuffling his sandalled feet,

"there's an old woman at the gate who says she must talk to you. At first she wanted to come in, and I had to point out that women aren't allowed inside monasteries. She said she knew that, but it was worth a try — the cheeky old creature! Then she ordered me, quite hoity-toity, to get you down to the gate straight away. Well! I told her that you're the bishop, and far too important to talk to every old person who passes by. And do you know, Father ..." — Wynt's eyes were popping with indignation — "she burst out laughing. And she won't go away."

Mungo breathed in sharply. His mouth felt dry and there was a tension round his heart that was half pain and half joy. Surely, he thought, there was only one person in the world who would be amused by Wynt's huffing and puffing about his importance?

"This old woman — what does she look like?" he asked.

Wynt stared.

"Like an old woman, Father," he replied.

Remembering that he was indeed a bishop, Mungo didn't skip down the glen like a little boy. He walked as a bishop should, with measured steps and his hands tucked decorously into his sleeves. Only when he opened the gate and saw Theneu, dignity deserted him. Not caring who saw him, he ran and threw his arms around her. Laughing and crying at the same time, they stood hugging each other in the middle of the road.

"You haven't changed at all," said Mungo a few days later, as he and Theneu sat in the autumn sunshine by a pool on the Mellendonor. Theneu was staying with Kedic's widow, Bera. It delighted Mungo that the two elderly women were already the best of friends.

"I didn't think bishops were supposed to tell lies," retorted Theneu, leaning forward to watch a trout slipping through the weedy green water. "I can see my reflection here, you know."

Mungo laughed. Of course Theneu had changed physically; her thin brown face had as many wrinkles as a withered apple, and her once abundant hair hung below her headcloth in two meagre grey plaits. Her body was bent by years of hard toil and her joints creaked with rheumatism. But her blue eyes were still bright and her serenity unruffled. She laughed a lot and was interested in everything.

"Ach, you know what I mean," Mungo said.

Mungo hadn't been surprised to hear that his messages had failed to reach Theneu. But he'd been amazed to learn that Serf was barely three months dead. Theneu said the old man had lost count of his own years, but she reckoned he was nearly a hundred.

"And after all, he didn't die at Cuilen Ros," she told Mungo. "He died miles away among his green hills. Actually, he'd been ill for ages, but he wouldn't give in."

"Maybe he didn't need you quite as much as you thought," suggested Mungo gently.

"He didn't need me at all," replied Theneu matter-of-factly. "I needed him."

She motioned to Mungo to help her to her feet. Arm in arm they walked through the trees, enjoying the chuckle of water and the vivid autumn leaves. High above the monastery, Theneu said she needed to sit down again.

"Old bones. Sorry," she grimaced.

"So — what now?" Mungo asked, watching as she made little boats with twigs and leaves and sent them whirling towards the waterfall.

Theneu paused and gave him a piercing blue look.

"Mungo," she said, as if he were still a little boy. "Why do you think I've come all this way, blistering my feet and

bruising my behind taking lifts on rickety farm carts? I
told you years ago. I'm going to found a convent. You're
going to make it happen."

So Mungo made it happen. In a sheltered spot beyond the
monastery fence, young monks built a small enclosure. In
it they erected a tiny church and cells for Theneu and
Bera, who wouldn't be parted from her new friend. Later
other women came, and the enclosure had to be enlarged.

Theneu was happy. She never told anyone that once
she'd been a princess, though as she grew older she
thought more often about her youth at Dun Paladyr. Not
that she brooded about cruel King Loth, or the vain,
greedy prince who was the father of her son — she had
forgiven them long ago. But when she heard the
monastery bell and smelt the rushes and lamp smoke in
the church, Theneu remembered the other little convent
on the windy hill, where she had first heard God's voice.
And she prayed for Sister Brignat, as she had done every
day of her life.

19. Queen Languoreth's Ring

"Bishop Mungo, I'd like to introduce you to my wife." Mungo hadn't forgotten his astonishment at King Rhydderch's words, or his misgiving when the king drew forward the wife he'd chosen after his victory at Arfderyyd. Lady Languoreth had pink cheeks, pale blue eyes and pretty, red-gold hair. She had simpered sweetly as she knelt on the grass at Hodelm to receive Mungo's blessing. It was easy to believe that her father, an unimportant prince, had been eager for an alliance with King Rhydderch. It was harder to believe that Languoreth, who was still in her teens, had been eager to marry a man almost old enough to be her grandfather.

For a while, however, King Rhydderch's marriage seemed to bring him happiness. Clearly the elderly husband doted on his young wife. Mungo wondered with mild amusement how Languoreth could walk under the weight of jewellery the king had given her. Most impressive was a gold ring, intricately wrought and inlaid with amber, which King Rhydderch presented on their second wedding anniversary. Sadly, trouble lay ahead.

Although his victory at Arfderyyd over his pagan enemies had been decisive, King Rhydderch still had problems to overcome. There were lawless tribes in the south, bandits in the north. To keep the peace he had to be away a lot, and because of danger he couldn't take Languoreth with him. The pretty, idle, uneducated young queen was left in the grim fortress at Alclut. While gales shrieked around the wooden walls and sucked at the thatch, she sat yawning and playing dice with her serving-women. Before long, she was looking for more perilous amusement.

Mungo, visiting Alclut one day in the king's absence, observed what was happening. Although he felt sorry for Languoreth, he spoke to her severely.

"You mustn't be so familiar with your husband's servants," he said. "Suppose someone told him how you're flirting with that young guard — Fearchar, isn't it? Think how hurt and angry the king would be. Have you no shame?"

Languoreth pouted and tossed her head.

"I'm sure I don't know what you mean, Bishop Mungo," she said. "I never flirt with anyone."

"Try not to tell lies," replied Mungo coldly. "Your behaviour is displeasing enough already, to God and to me."

That afternoon, with a heavy heart, Mungo trudged homeward through sleet. A week later, word came that King Rhydderch was back. Another week passed before Mungo heard the next part of the story.

"Father." On a wintry morning Anguen poked his head into the writing-room, where Mungo was busy copying a psalm-book for Conval's church at Rhynfrwd. "Sorry to disturb you, but Queen Languoreth's at the gate. She says please may she speak to you urgently."

Mungo stopped blowing on his numb fingers and got down from his stool.

"Take the queen over to the convent church, Brother," he said. "Her servants can wait in the porch."

It was when Anguen said, "She has no servants," that Mungo knew this was serious. Queens didn't normally travel alone.

In the flickering lamplight of Theneu's little church, Mungo peered at Languoreth's strained, frightened face.

She was shivering violently under her fur-trimmed cloak.

"My child, this time you had better tell me the truth," he said.

After what he'd witnessed at Alclut, nothing in Languoreth's story surprised Mungo. On the night of Rhydderch's return, after a long day's riding, he had fallen into a doze at the table. Fancying that he was fast asleep, Languoreth had thought it safe to flirt and giggle with Fearchar. As the evening went on she had, she admitted, drunk too much wine. Towards midnight, in an act of incredible folly, she had slipped King Rhydderch's precious ring onto the young man's finger.

"Next morning I was sorry I'd given away my nice ring," said Languoreth, trying to control her trembling lip, "but I wasn't really worried. My husband was as kind as ever, so I assumed he didn't know what I'd done. Then, the day before yesterday, Fearchar didn't come to play dice with me. So I went to the guard-room to look for him."

"And?" prompted Mungo.

Tears of terror filled Languoreth's blue eyes.

"He wasn't there," she whispered. "I looked everywhere and couldn't find him. Oh, Bishop Mungo, Fearchar has run away, and he must have taken my ring."

Mungo repressed a sigh, but he said nothing. After much sniffing, Languoreth managed to go on.

"Last night at supper, my husband said,Tell me, my dear, where is that gold ring I gave you on our anniversary? I hope it isn't too heavy for your pretty little finger?' I ... I told a lie, Bishop Mungo."

"Not for the first time," Mungo reminded her. "What did you say, Languoreth?"

"I said,Oh no, sire. I must have forgotten to put it on.' My husband said,Then let me see you wearing it when we meet for supper tomorrow evening.'" Languoreth had sunk down on her knees. Her nose was scarlet and now tears were streaming down her cheeks.

"Oh, what shall I do?" she sobbed. "When I can't produce the ring King Rhydderch will kill me, or shut me up in a place like this. I don't want to die and I'd hate being a nun!"

I don't suppose your sister-nuns would be too keen either, thought Mungo, imagining Theneu's face. For the first time, he was tempted to smile.

"What do you want me to do?" he asked patiently. "Speak to the king on your behalf?"

"No! I want you to work a miracle," Languoreth howled.

Mungo shook his head. He thought he'd never heard anything so pathetically childish in his life. But as he looked at the slight, quaking figure at his feet, it occurred to him that that was what Languoreth was — pathetic and childish. His exasperation gave way to pity.

With God's help, I can get her out of this mess, he thought, and do King Rhydderch a favour too. It won't break my rule of only using my power to help the suffering. Mungo closed his eyes and asked God to tell him where the ring was. As soon as God answered, Mungo knew what to do.

"Languoreth," Mungo said. "If I help you, shall I have your solemn promise to be a faithful wife in future? Your husband is a good man, and he loves you."

"Yes, I know. I'm very, very sorry," cried Languoreth.

"Go down to the village and find a fisherman," Mungo told her. "Tell him to cast a line into the clear water of the Clut. He will catch a salmon and in its mouth you will find your ring."

Languoreth didn't wait to ask questions. Scrambling to her feet, she hitched her dress above her knees. Mungo watched her sprinting out of the church and across the grass. By the time he reached the gate, she had disappeared among the trees at the foot of the glen.

Mungo wouldn't have minded being a fly on the wall that night, when Languoreth walked into the hall at Alclut wearing the precious ring. He couldn't help smiling as he imagined King Rhydderch goggling in disbelief. For although he didn't yet understand all that had happened, it seemed to Mungo improbable that a poor soldier like Fearchar had thrown a valuable ring into the Clut. I wonder what Rhydderch's been up to, he thought. Another week passed, however, before Mungo's curiosity was satisfied.

It was a moist, misty morning when the King at last rode up to the monastery gate. After Wynt had taken charge of his horse, he sat down with Mungo on the dining-room porch.

"I hear you've gone into the fishing business," said Rhydderch, cocking an eyebrow at his friend.

"Who on earth told you that?" asked Mungo, who thought that his advice to Languoreth was a secret.

"My wife," Rhydderch told him, adding rather proudly, "She said she wanted to confess everything, so that we could have a fresh start together."

"Good for her," said Mungo approvingly. Then he took a chance. "Did *you* have anything to confess?" he asked.

Rhydderch looked startled, but then he shrugged.

"I didn't see any point," he said. "But I don't mind telling you."

"Go on, then," Mungo replied.

"I know it hasn't been easy for Languoreth," the King began, "being married to an old man like me. For a long time I turned a blind eye to her flirting, but when one night I saw her giving my ring to a young guard called Fearchar, I realized I was being made to look ridiculous.

So I decided to teach them both a lesson."

"It was time," Mungo agreed.

"My opportunity came the next day," continued the King, "when I took my guards out hunting. When we stopped to eat and rest by the river, there was young Fearchar, as bold as brass, with my wife's ring on his finger. I could have killed him, of course, but I'm sick of slaughter and besides, Languoreth was much to blame. So I waited until everyone had settled down for a nap, then I tiptoed over to Fearchar and drew the ring off his finger. I intended to put it in my pocket, but suddenly it was hateful to me. I wanted rid of it, so I threw it into the Clut."

"Then it was you. I thought it might have been," said Mungo. "Fearchar must have got a fright when he woke up."

The sudden twisting of Rhydderch's features showed how much he had been hurt.

"At first the rascal was up in arms," he said contemptuously, "thinking that one of his fellow-guards had robbed him. Then he caught my eye, and the truth dawned. For the rest of the day I watched him sweating, wondering when I was going to pounce. When darkness fell, he took the coward's way and fled."

Mungo sat in silence for a while, watching the mist drifting over the fence. At length he said, "I think you did right to let him go. But what about Queen Languoreth? Suppose I hadn't been able to help her? If she'd come to supper without the ring, would you have punished her?"

The King shook his head.

"She's been punished enough," he said. "But if she hadn't been persuaded by the miracle to tell me the truth, I'd never have been able to trust her again."

"So I did right too?" asked Mungo.

"You did, and I'm forever grateful," Rhydderch replied.

20. An Important Visitor

Queen Languoreth kept her word. She was kind and loving to her husband for the rest of their life together. In the spring of the following year, she and Rhydderch had a baby boy whom Mungo baptized Constantin. King Rhydderch had every reason to be a happy man, but he wasn't. Mungo was very worried about him and so was the queen.

"I think the memory of his battle against Hueil at Arfderyyd is preying on Rhydderch's mind," Languoreth told Mungo, who had called in at Alclut to see the baby. "I've heard the slaughter was ghastly enough to turn anybody's wits. So many years on the run couldn't have been good for his nerves either," she added with a sigh.

"Has he spoken at all?" asked Mungo anxiously.

Languoreth nodded.

"He's got it into his head that he's going to be ambushed and killed," she said. "He's taken to wearing padded tunics, and he can't walk down a passage in his own house without twitching and looking over his shoulder. It's getting us all down, but there's no reasoning with him."

Constantin began to howl. Mungo, who was bouncing him on his knee, hastily returned him to Languoreth.

"I've got to go to Perdeyc today," he said, "and business may keep me there the rest of the week. I'll come and see King Rhydderch on Monday. Maybe I can talk some sense into him."

Meanwhile, however, the king had another visitor. Far away in the west, on an island called Hy, there lived an Irish abbot called Columba. Like Mungo, he travelled widely, preaching the Gospel and founding churches. For a while, Columba had worked mainly among his own people, settlers who had named their new homeland Dal Riata, after the place in Ireland from which they'd come. Later Columba had extended his activities into Pictland, and recently monks from Hy had been working in the British kingdom of Alclut.

When he'd first heard this, Mungo hadn't been altogether pleased. The Britons were his people, after all. Eventually, though, he'd decided that he didn't mind; if the Gospel was preached, it was unimportant who did the preaching. Mungo had made friends with Lugne Mocumin, a Pictish monk who was a follower of Columba, and had introduced him to King Rhydderch. While Mungo was away at Perdeyc, Lugne called in at Alclut. He too was shocked to find Rhydderch a nervous wreck.

"Listen, my lord King," said Lugne, looking earnestly at Rhydderch with his shining dark eyes. "My advice is to consult Columba. He has the gift of seeing into the future. If anyone can set your mind at rest, he can."

Rhydderch got up and crept to the door. When he had made sure no one was listening outside, he crept back.

"Will you take a message to him from me?" he whispered.

"No need," said Lugne. "Columba intends to visit Mungo at Glasgu next month. You can talk to him yourself."

When Mungo heard that Columba was planning to visit Glasgu, he was as thrilled as a child. Columba was a legend in his own lifetime; even in an age when most monks encountered some danger, Columba's escapades were hair-raising. Mungo knew that Columba was a prince in Ireland, who'd been given by his parents to serve the church. This hadn't stopped him from behaving haughtily, quarrelling with the High King and instigating a battle in which three thousand men had died. It didn't seem proper behaviour for a man whose Irish name, Colm cille, meant "the Dove of the church."

Of course, Columba had realized this. Stricken with remorse, he had left his beloved Ireland to found a monastery on bleak, lonely Hy. But before long he'd been off to the mainland, having adventures again. Red-haired and flamboyant, he'd survived storms at sea and overpowered whales and wild animals. He'd outsmarted druids and performed miracles all over Pictland. Most spectacular had been his encounter with an enormous water-serpent, bent on eating Lugne Mocumin as he swam in the river at Inbhear Nesa.

"I've never seen anything so awesome in my life," Lugne had told Mungo. "The beast was so long that its head was in the river and the end of its scaly green tail half way down the loch. It had rolling red eyes and a forked tongue and fangs like knives. I thought I was done for, until Columba jumped into the water and made the sign of the Cross in front of the brute's slobbering jaws.Get back into the loch, monster,' he roared.Leave this man alone!'"

"And did it — get back?" Mungo had asked, wide-eyed.

"Of course," said Lugne, "otherwise I wouldn't be here now. It hissed and spat and lashed its tail until the loch boiled, but Columba stared it out. Eventually it stood right up on its tail, screamed and dived. There were monks fainting all over the place, I can tell you."

And this, thought Mungo, is the man who's coming to stay with me!

"We have a month to prepare," he said. "Everything must be perfect to receive the monks from Hy."

Lugne had told Mungo to expect a company of two hundred. Mungo had gone pale at the thought, but the organization hadn't proved too difficult. Blankets were borrowed to make temporary sleeping places. A huge quantity of bread was baked, eggs were hoarded and cheese stored.

"Everyone will wear a clean habit," said Mungo, "and most of you need a haircut. If Lugne Mocumin is an example, I don't think the Hy monks will be particularly spruce. Still, we want to look our best."

As the week in which Columba was expected approached, the anticipation at Glasgu rose almost to fever pitch. Mungo would have been annoyed with his monks if he hadn't shared their excitement. At long last, on a placid summer afternoon, Clynog came running to announce that a procession of brown-clad monks was approaching from the west.

"They'll be here in half an hour," he gasped.

"Ring the bell to welcome them," ordered Mungo.

There was chaos for ten minutes as Telleyr and Anguen tried to get the monks into line. Wynt scurried up and down, imploring people to tie their belts neatly and straighten their sleeves. At last everyone was ready — just in time. As the clear notes of the bell died away, the sound of singing was heard outside the gate.

"The saints shall go from strength to strength! Hallelujah!"

"Altogether, now — one, two!" whispered Mungo, opening the gate.

"How great is the glory of the Lord!" sang the Glasgu monks, as Mungo's procession and Columba's moved towards each other over the grass. Mungo only had eyes for the tall, hawk-nosed, elderly man whose keen grey eyes were fixed on him.

"Columba, welcome to Glasgu," he said warmly. "Welcome to you all!"

That evening, a feast was held on the green bank outside the monastery fence. Columba, Mungo and their most senior monks shared a long table. Everyone else sat on the grass. Mungo couldn't help feeling proud of his white-robed monks as they glided among their brown-robed guests, offering dishes of salmon and eggs. Bread and honey, apples and cheese were also passed round. The monks, who rarely attended a party, were well content. Afterwards, as the setting sun burnished the river, all the brothers worshipped God together. It had been a wonderful day.

"Brother, I'd like to ask you something," said Mungo to Wynt, before they went to bed. Mungo had given up his own cell to Columba, and was going to sleep out of doors. "Would it grieve you terribly if I gave Abbot Columba the shepherd's crook you carved for me? I want to give him a wonderful present, and the crook is my greatest treasure."

A blush of pleasure rose on Wynt's thin cheeks.

"Father! I shall be honoured," he said.

Columba stayed with Mungo for several days, and they had many long talks together. Sometimes Mungo found his position lonely, and he was glad to confide in someone who shared the joys and disappointments of trying to convert the unbelieving. He told Columba about his childhood at Cuilen Ros, and about the bulls and the white boar. He reminisced about his happy years at Llanelwy.

"I've had an interesting life," he said, "though not as spectacular as yours, by all accounts."

"I dare say accounts have been exaggerated," laughed Columba. "Anyway, I lead a quieter life nowadays."

On the day when Columba went off to Alclut to help King Rhydderch deal with his problem, Mungo felt at a loose end. Sadly, he realized how much he'd miss his new friend when he was gone.

It was a Saturday when Columba left. There were sad faces among the Glasgu brothers, and among the monks from Hy as they prepared for their long journey. They felt like children whose long-anticipated treat was too quickly over. In a little ceremony at the gate, Mungo presented his crook to Columba. To his surprise and delight, he received in return Columba's crook, lovingly carved and polished by a monk on Hy. Then they said goodbye.

Clynog rang the monastery bell as the long brown procession moved off down river towards the sea. He went on ringing it, even after it began to rain, until he was sure that Columba and his friends could hear it no more.

21. Myrddin the Wizard

On a shining spring morning when the leaves were tender and the dippers building their nests in the grey rock, Mungo climbed to a still pool at the head of the glen. He had never wasted time looking at himself but now, on impulse, he leant over the water and stared hard at his reflection. He saw a thin, deeply lined face with blue eyes screwed up because they didn't see as well as they used to. What was left of the once golden hair was white and, alas, there was a lack of teeth. Like Serf before him, Mungo had lost count of his own years, but that he was old was undeniable.

In many ways, the twelve years since Columba's visit had been good. King Rhydderch, reassured by Columba that he would die at home on his own pillow, had thrown away his padded tunics. Bright and confident once more, he had ruled his kingdom wisely and well. Because there was peace, the people prospered. Farms produced more food and the roads were safer. The church was flourishing in all but a few, isolated places.

Personally, Mungo had known sadness. Theneu had died at a great age and had been buried beside a burn she loved. More recently Columba, who had kept in close touch, had died on his island of Hy. Inevitably these deaths made Mungo consider his own. I suppose I should be slowing down, he thought, and giving younger brothers more responsibility. At the same time he felt restless, as he always did in spring.

"I think I'll go away for a while," Mungo said to his friends a day or two later. "I'll walk up the Clut to the ford, then go cross-country into the Wood of Celidon. I need to be by myself," he added, seeing Wynt open his mouth to protest.

"But will you be safe, Father?" asked Caet, a young monk who didn't know Mungo very well.

Mungo shrugged slightly.

"As safe as I've ever been," he replied.

Safe or not, Mungo had never felt happier than when he crossed the Clut and began to tramp eastward among hills bearded with trees. In the valleys, everything was fresh and green with the promise of summer. Streams gushed and the sun drew liquid patterns on the damp forest floor. Mungo couldn't walk far without rest these days, but he was in no hurry. Kindly woodlanders gave him food and sometimes shelter. The nights he enjoyed most were those he spent in the open. Lying wrapped in his cloak, he listened to owls hooting and a vixen's eerie yelp. He enjoyed the scampering of mice and the tiny grunts of hedgehogs. Through lacy holes in the branches he watched the eternal stars.

As the days grew warmer and hawthorn blossom scented the air, Mungo wandered deeper into the forest. The trees crowded one another and the net of branches admitted less light. But when it rained, he was protected from all but drips.

It was a damp, rather chilly morning when Mungo first sensed he wasn't alone. The forest was full of noises, and for a while he tried to convince himself that the snapping of twigs and rustling of bushes had natural causes. Yet, as the day passed, Mungo became more and more certain that eyes were watching him.

"Who's there? Why don't you come out?" he called, but the trees muffled his voice and there was no reply.

That night, Mungo lay down in the lee of a rock beside a swift-running burn. He had never again felt the kind of fear he'd experienced, alone in the fog, on his way to Cymru, but he was cold and couldn't help feeling on edge. For the first time he missed his friends. He didn't sleep much, but the night passed quietly.

In the morning, when he'd bathed and said his prayers, Mungo set off down the burn bank. On one side the wood was dense, on the other straggly, like thinning hair. It wasn't long before Mungo again knew that he was being watched. Towards noon he glimpsed someone dodging among the dense trees.

"Come on out," he called across the water. "Why are you so afraid?"

There was a pause. Then suddenly there erupted from the wood the most extraordinary figure Mungo had ever seen. Naked apart from a scrap of animal skin covering his loins, the man was filthy, with a matted beard and wild black hair hanging almost to his waist. Crouching like an animal he faced Mungo across the burn. Mungo could hear him snuffling and making little whimpering noises. His pale eyes were crazed with fear. Mungo felt nothing except overwhelming pity.

"What's your name?" he called gently. "Will you come over, or shall I cross to you?"

The second question was answered first. With an enormous leap the wild man cleared the burn. Trembling, he fell on his knees at Mungo's feet.

"My name is Myrddin," he whispered hoarsely. "I saw you coming before you left the holy place. I see things inside my head," he added pathetically.

"So do I, sometimes," said Mungo, "though I didn't see you. Come and sit down, Myrddin. I want to hear your story."

Mungo's voice seemed to soothe Myrddin. He allowed himself to be drawn to a sheltered spot on the bank. Mungo unrolled his cloak and put it round the poor man's shoulders.

"I haven't much time," croaked Myrddin, rolling his colourless eyes. "It's foretold that I must die three times, by falling, hanging and drowning. Now the assassins hired by my old master, King Meldred, are closing in. Have you heard of Arfderyyd?" he asked abruptly.

Mungo nodded. Everyone had heard of the battle where King Rhydderch and his allies had defeated their pagan enemies. It had been so bloody that, according to Queen Languoreth, it had preyed on Rhydderch's mind.

"I was there," said Myrddin. "Oh, don't look so surprised, good man. I haven't always been as I am now. Once I was a great and powerful wizard, known throughout the land for my gift of prophecy. I was King Meldred's magician. You've heard of King Meldred?"

Mungo repressed a shudder. He had certainly heard of King Meldred, a murderous associate of Hueil and Caw. Unlike them, he had survived the battle at Arfderyyd, and for years had stirred up trouble for Rhydderch in the south of his kingdom. Tales of Meldred's cruelty made the blood run cold.

"You had an evil master," said Mungo, but Myrddin was intent on his story.

"I too lived like a king," he said. "I had palaces, golden ornaments, chariots and fine clothes. But pride caused my downfall. When King Meldred and his allies consulted me, I told them to stake everything on one battle with the Christians. Protected by my magic spells, I boasted, they would be invincible." Myrddin sat silent for a moment, his face twisted with pain. Then he took a deep breath and went on. "I rode with the kings to the killing ground, proud in my saffron robes and with a circlet of silver on my brow. Calling on the gods, I chanted my spells, taunting and cursing our enemies. But ... but ..."

"The spells didn't work," Mungo said.

Myrddin shook his head.

"It was terrible," he whispered. "I'd never seen a battle before, only heard of noble deeds and glorious victory. It wasn't like that at all. All around me war-horns bellowed and the clang of weapons drowned my futile prayers. I saw headless corpses and young boys maimed and dying in pools of blood. And there were horses, mortally wounded. Oh, Mungo ..." — He knows my name, Mungo thought — "I was so ashamed and so afraid. But there was worse to come."

"Tell me."

"I shall." Myrddin's black-nailed fingers crept out and touched Mungo's hand. "When the battle was almost over," he said, "when the winners were cheering and the losers were weeping and counting the slain, the clouds above my head were torn open. A great wind arose, and carried on it I heard a voice.Myrddin,' it said,your pride and folly have caused this slaughter. Now you must be punished. You will live in the forest like a beast among beasts, pursued by those who hate you, until your life ends.'"

Myrddin paused, shivering uncontrollably. "Then my head was pierced by a terrible brightness," he sobbed. "The sky blazed and troops of fiery warriors swooped down on me, hissing and brandishing their spears. Was it your God's voice I heard? Am I to burn in hell for ever?"

"I don't think so." Aching with pity, Mungo put a comforting arm round Myrddin. "When I hear God's voice," he said quietly, "it often tells me what I already know deep down — that I've done something wrong and that I must show I'm sorry. You weren't the only person to blame for the battle, but you're the only one who's repented and suffered for his part in it. Am I right?"

"Oh, yes," sobbed Myrddin.

"Then my God has already forgiven you," said Mungo. "He knows all you've endured. Heaven is very near."

"What happened next?" asked Anguen.

It was late on a warm July evening. The old group of friends had gathered outside Mungo's cell to welcome him home. To their delight, he was in the mood for traveller's tales.

"Did the poor wizard recover his wits?" Telleyr wanted to know.

Mungo sighed.

"I think he did," he said, "though he didn't live long enough for it to make much difference. God forgive me, I thought his talk of assassins and a triple death were sick delusions, but there was truth in them after all."

"Did you baptize him, Father?" asked Clynog anxiously.

"Yes," nodded Mungo. "Down by the burn I blessed the water and poured some on his head.'Your sins are forgiven,' I said,in Christ's name.' For the first time the poor man smiled, and I think he knew a moment of peace. But before I could speak again, there was shouting and crashing among the trees. Myrddin jumped up and bounded away down the bank like a hunted deer. A group of ruffians — five or six, armed with clubs and staves —leapt out of the wood and rushed after him. I didn't see the end, thank God."

"But what about the triple death, Father?" asked Wynt, looking puzzled. "Can anyone die three times?"

"No. Once is enough," said Mungo gently. "Yet there was truth in Myrddin's prophecy. Later in the day, I reached a fishing village where the burn met a greater river called Twyd. There I learned what had happened. As his pursuers closed in on him, Myrddin leapt from a high rock into the river. Underneath there were stakes supporting salmon nets. The poor wretch fell among the nets and was suspended, head down in the water. Before the fishermen could cut him free, he drowned. Falling, hanging and drowning, just as he said," concluded Mungo. "But only one death for each of us, Brother Wynt."

22. Epiphany

After his journey to the Wood of Celidon, Mungo didn't want to travel any more. He was too stiff, too tired, too old. As the last seasons of his life flitted by, he left the running of the monastery to his younger brothers and retreated to his cell. Sitting at the door he scattered crumbs of bread for the birds; he didn't notice that he ate less and less himself. His body shrank until it resembled a bundle of sticks inside his white habit. The younger monks worried about him.

For Mungo, it was one of God's greatest blessings that his four closest companions had been spared to share his old age. Five tottering old greybeards, they still prayed together every day. Clynog, who had the best eyesight, helped Wynt, who was nearly blind. Telleyr, who had the strongest legs, fetched food from the kitchen for the rest. Anguen, always known for his sense of humour, could still make everyone laugh.

"It would be wonderful if God allowed us to die together," said Wynt wistfully.

He could scarcely bear to think of being left in the world without Mungo, and secretly Mungo felt the same about him. However detached he became from the rest of the world, Mungo never stopped thanking God for giving him these friends, and for allowing him to keep them for so long.

One year, after an autumn spoiled by rain and spiteful winds, winter came cruelly. Christmas was dark and dreary, with sleet gusting through the glen. January began with a blizzard; on the fifth day the snow half melted, but overnight the thaw was cut dead by bitter frost. Grass stiffened, puddles glassed over and the waterfall hung in a silent suspension of ice.

"We must get Father Mungo and the other old ones into the kitchen where it's warm," said Brother Caet, who was now more or less in charge. "None of them is long for this world, but we can't let them freeze to death."

"No, we can't," agreed the others.

But when Caet climbed the frozen glen to Mungo's cell, Mungo was having none of it.

"When I got back from the church on Christmas Day," he said, "I decided not to leave my cell again. Don't worry, Brother Caet. I'm perfectly all right."

Caet peered through the gloom at the frail old body on the bed of stone. Mungo's hollow cheeks were blue, but under his blanket cloak he had stopped shivering. Caet knew this was a bad sign.

"Then let me bring some sheepskins, Father," pleaded the young man. "It would be so easy to make you more comfortable."

"I am comfortable. Go away," Mungo said.

In one sense, despite the cold, Mungo was comfortable. He knew that he was dying at last, and he really wanted to be left in peace to get on with it. He didn't feel lonely; since Christmas, he'd been aware of other presences in his little cell. Several times he'd had visions of angels which had filled him with joy. What did cold nights matter to him now, when he was on the brink of a morning of ineffable happiness and light?

And yet... as he lay in the dark, listening to Caet's retreating footsteps, it occurred to Mungo that he was being unkind. Should he leave his brothers feeling guilty because he had died alone, unhappy because they'd been denied the chance to show him kindness at the end? And what of Wynt and his other faithful friends? Mungo knew that if he refused to come to the kitchen for the warm bath, blankets and hot milk which Caet had offered, they would refuse too. Would God deny them a little comfort after such long, self-denying lives? Of course not. Then Mungo couldn't either.

As he lay waiting for Caet to return, the voices of monks singing drifted up to Mungo from the church. He recognized the hymns for the feast of Epiphany, when three kings from the east had brought precious gifts to the Christ Child. As a little boy, Mungo had liked that story though Theneu, for some forgotten reason, hadn't had much time for kings. She had insisted that the gift most pleasing to God was the gift of oneself to others. Just for a moment, Mungo had been in danger of forgetting that.

Mungo hadn't expected dying to be such a friendly experience. When Brother Caet carried him carefully into the kitchen, he saw that his four companions were already there. They were lying near the fire on sheepskins, propped up on bales of soft wool. An enormous bowl, normally used to collect rainwater, had been placed in the middle of the floor. Four young monks, with their sleeves rolled up, were filling it with jugs of hot water. Their fresh, rounded faces were solemn, but Mungo could tell how proud they were to have been chosen for this important task.

"You first, Father," said Caet briskly.

Mungo allowed himself to be undressed and put into the bath. There was just room for him to sit with his knees drawn up. Gently Caet poured warm water over him and chafed his frozen hands and feet. Gradually, feeling returned to them.

When Mungo had been dried and wrapped in blankets, he watched his friends being given the same treatment. It was clear now that God intended to grant Wynt's prayer that they should all die together; although Anguen could still summon a smile and Wynt whisper, "God bless you," Mungo doubted that any of them really knew what was going on. When everyone had been bathed, the young monks put the aged ones to bed and brought them cups of hot milk. Mungo hated hot milk, but he drank it anyway. The unaccustomed warmth made him drowsy and soon he fell asleep.

For a week, Mungo drifted in and out of consciousness. He was dimly aware of kind hands and voices, and knew that his friends were nearby. Sometimes he thought he was a little boy playing on the shore at Cuilen Ros. Sometimes he thought he was at Llanelwy, walking with King Maelgwyn Gwynedd in the soft summer rain. He called Caet "Asaph."

"Listen to our brothers singing in the church, Asaph, my son," he said.

The Lord knows what we are made of;
he remembers that we are dust...
But for those who honour the Lord,
His love lasts for ever.

On 13 January, Mungo died, followed swiftly by Telleyr, Anguen, Clynog and Wynt. The monks who had looked after them wrapped their bodies in fine linen and carried them to the church. The following day, in thin winter sunshine, they buried them together in the same grave.

Endnote

After Mungo died, many grieving friends came to visit his grave. It wasn't long before stories began to circulate of sick people being cured there. Soon Glasgu became, and remained for hundreds of years, a place of pilgrimage. These are the words of Mungo's twelfth-century biographer, Joscelin of Furness:

> When the spirit of St Kentigern had been taken up to the starry realms, the Earth took his body back into herself. But the power of miracles which he had possessed when alive now burst forth. At his tomb sight is restored to the blind, hearing to the deaf, the power of walking to the lame, strength of limb to the paralysed, a sound mind to the mentally ill, speech to the dumb and cleanness of skin to lepers.

Place names

In Mungo's time, many places and rivers had names different from those they have today. Here are some of the places mentioned in this book and their modern counterparts.

In Scotland:

Aberlessic	Aberlady
Alclut	Dumbarton
Celidon	Caledon
Clut	Clyde
Cuilen Ros	Culross
Dun Paladyr	Dumpelder (Traprain Law)
Glasgu	Glasgow
Gwerid	Forth
Hodelm	Hoddam
Hy	Iona
Inbhear Nesa	Inverness
Kernach	Carnock
Mellendonor	Molendinar
Perdeyc	Partick
Rhynfrwd	Renfrew
Sulwath	Solway
Twyd	Tweed

In Cumbria:

Arfderyyd	Arthuret
Caer Luel	Carlisle

In Wales (Cymru):

Llanelwy	St Asaph
Mynyw	St David's

The Queen of the Silver Castle

Claire French

Pwyll, King of Dyfed, is hunting in the Red Forest when he sees a magnificent stag through the mist. In the heat of the chase Pwyll strays beyond the standing stones that mark the boundary with the Kingdom of Annwn, and is brought face to face with the Grey Hunter.

Disguised as each other, they exchange identities, and Pwyll enters the Otherworld as the mighty Grey Hunter with the task of defeating King Havgan in single combat.

Pwyll's adventures lead him to encounters with the Druids, ancient magic and consequences for his own Kingdom of Dyfed.

This book beautifully retells the stories from the Red Book of Hergest, which itself is just one of the Celtic manuscripts that form the Welsh epic *The Mabinogion*.

Floris Books